MATTERS OF

Kindness

by

Terry Belleville

Unless otherwise stated, this is a work of fiction. Names, characters, places, and incidents are either the products of the author's imagination. Any resemblance to actual persons, living or dead, events, or locales is entirely coincidental.

The Factory Inc., Canada

ISBN 978-0-9949469-2-8

Available from Amazon.com,
Createspace.com, and other retail outlets.

terrybelleville.com

Dedication

This work would not have been possible without
the tireless support and encouragement of my
wife, Donna Belleville, and of our sons Jason and Ryan.
Their zest for life and their love of laughter keep me young.
Special thanks to Doug Reid for his keen eye,
and his appreciation of good beer.

Content

Going to the Dogs.

This was a time when nature was cruel, life was uncluttered, and friendship meant everything.

Just standing on the side of the street outside the hotel, Rabbit, a short scrubby, dusty, little man, could feel the perspiration trickling down his back. His faded blue jacket couldn't blot any more sweat. The half dozen corks dangling from his stained hat helped keep the sticky black flies out of his eyes. The heat was merciless, like so many days in December had been that year.

He joined his mate, Dodger, who had been sitting on the bench outside the hotel with his dog, Ginger, stretched out beside him. Dodger was a life-long friend who lived near Rabbit in Mansfield, a small country town northeast of Melbourne. Dodger was considerably taller than Rabbit and had more teeth. The men acknowledged each other with nods. It was just too hot to speak.

The 1920s through the 1930s had proven to be the driest period in Australia over the previous four centuries. According to measurements at the Mansfield Post Office, November of 1939 yielded less than a quarter inch of rain in the whole month; December followed suit. When temperatures consistently hovered around the century mark, the earth became so hard-baked that any precious precipitation that did land ran off quickly before it had any chance to seep into the ground.

Molly Brennan, the publican's wife came out of the hotel with a large bowl of water. She placed it on the ground beside Ginger. The dog raised her head and looked at her.

"What are you looking at, Ginger? Eh?" said Molly. The dog panted, and her long, pink tongue lolled out the side of her mouth. "I brought you a drink, old girl." With the grace of a small foal, Ginger struggled to her feet. Molly cupped Ginger's face in her hands and used her thumbs to gently stroke the dog's face. "You should take better care of her. If she needs water, you should come into the pub and get it. Don't wait for me to do it for you." The remark was not blatantly directed at Dodger but was more of a general admonishment to the two men. Molly looked toward a swirl of black smoke off to the west. "Don't like the look of that? More than a few acres going up in smoke there," she said. Don't know if that's this morning's or hanging over from last night." The three of them studied eddies of smoke that rose into the still air.

"What do you think, Rabbit?" asked Molly. "This going to last?"

Rabbit looked to the edges of the horizon as if he could somehow see beyond. Then he cocked his head, listening to the sound of the earth or anything that dwelt upon it. "You know what I reckon?" he said finally.

"What?" asked Dodger as he watched a truck recede down the street into a pall of red dust.

"Gonna be hot," said Rabbit.

"You reckon?" said Dodger.

"Bloody hot."

"It's already bloody hot," said Dodger.

"He's got a point there," said Molly as she casually stroked Ginger's dusty coat. "When are we going to see rain do you think?"

"Don't hold ya breath," said Rabbit.

Rabbit crouched down and picked up some red dirt that he rubbed between his hands like a herb he hoped to savor. "Remember the terrible bushfires we had back in the nineties, remember them?" he said.

"My oath," said Dodger.

Rabbit cupped his hands around his nose, sampling the scent. "This one could be worse. A lot worse."

"We should pray for rain," said Dodger.

"Worth a shot," said Rabbit. "We'll make that your job."

The three of them fell silent watching for whatever stirred on that oppressive Sunday morning.

The only sound to be heard was Ginger lapping water from the bowl. "Who's the good girl? Having a lovely drink is she?" said Dodger as he fondly stroked the dog.

"You've changed your tune, Dodger," said Molly. "I remember you saying a dog was, if I remember correctly, just a bloody nuisance. You'd never want one."

"Nah, doesn't ring a bell," said Dodger as he continued to stroke Ginger.

Rabbit had rescued Ginger from an abusive owner. She had been so neglected and mistreated that she couldn't walk. Rabbit found her lying on the side of the road where she had either fallen out of or been thrown from a truck. He carried the dog in his arms for almost two miles before Norm Clancy happened upon them and brought them home.

"You may never get her back now, Rabbit," said Molly. "She's obviously taken a shine to Dodger." Molly smiled at the obvious affection the old codger had for the dog.

Rabbit lovingly nursed the emaciated dog back to health. He had seriously intended to keep her but felt his mate, Dodger, might have a greater need of companionship.

A couple of months prior, Dodger's best mate, Tom, was chopping wood as a favour for Nettie Kelly, a frail widow who lived nearby. It was unreasonably hot. Not a good day to be exerting that sort of effort. Tom had a heart attack, and although Nettie called the hospital straight away, the damage was done.

Dodger made it to the hospital to be with Tom that very afternoon. When he asked if he could do anything, Tom said yes there was something, so Dodger left the hospital to finish chopping the wood for Nettie.

He went back to see Tom shortly after dinner and took a pack of cards with him. He asked Tom if he felt up to it. Tom said yes as long as Dodger didn't cheat. They had a good laugh about that.

Cards had been a ritual in their lives for as long as they could remember. They would sit for hours playing cards, having a beer or two and swearing at each other. Dodger felt a game of euchre would lift Tom's spirits; it was his favourite. Tom was a canny player and generally had the best of Dodger. Not so much that evening, he was tired and had trouble staying focused on the game.

"I really should go, Tom, you need your rest." It was not the first time Dodger had said that.

"No, don't go, mate. One more hand."

"That's what you said last time, and you fell asleep."

"Didn't."

"Yes, you did, mate."

"Silly bugger." Tom smiled, settled back and closed his eyes again.

"One more hand, and then I'm gonna go for sure," said Dodger.

"I just..." The thought hung in the air. Tom shook his head slightly, a little annoyed that his senses had betrayed him. He raised his hand to see if it could somehow grasp the sentence from the air. "Sorry."

"No worries, mate."

Dodger gathered up the cards. It was odd to see his friend from that angle in that light in that sterile place. It was odd to see him so passive. Any other day, when Tom squinted through his bushy silver brows, there was a spark, a curiosity, and an interest in how things were and how they got to be that way. That night just holding the cards was a challenge. How Dodger wanted Tom to look at him in that old way and call him a silly bugger one more time.

"Tom?"

"What?" It was more of a whisper than a word.

"Nothin'."

Tom looked older than Dodger thought either of them would ever be. "You want me to deal?" Tom responded with the faintest smile and a hint of a nod. "Right. I'll deal. I'll give 'em a good shuffle, too," said Dodger. "You always tell me I don't know how to shuffle. Let's see how I do this time, eh?"

He did what he had promised. He gave them a good shuffle dealt out two hands. "Look at that, mate," said Dodger with a laugh. "A right bower. Dealt myself a right bower and you said I couldn't shuffle."

Tom didn't reach for his cards. The air had become very still around them.

"Tom?" Dodger said, in a faint hope that his friend was still there. Dodger stayed by Tom's bedside until a nurse came by on her rounds. He didn't want his mate to be alone.

It was shortly after losing Tom that Rabbit felt Dodger should have his dog.

Dodger wasn't too sure.

Rabbit said it would help.

He was right.

The Man at the Counter.

Learning a lesson that shaped my life.

Dad kept a mulga wood bowl beside his bed for small change. It was a swirl of pennies, halfpennies, threepenny and sixpenny pieces and, on the odd glorious occasion, a shilling. The bowl served two purposes. One was obvious, to find a home for dad's clutter of coins. The other was to give my brother and me occasional access to money without actually having to ask for it.

There was an unspoken rule: access to the privilege could not be abused by overindulgence and the monies could not be wasted on anything frivolous. That only had to be said once. We clearly understood. As I reflect upon it, I think it is interesting that there was never any articulated consequence to be rendered should either of us transgress. Dad just assumed we wouldn't. He was right.

I used my pennies exclusively for critical and discreet needs, like the cost of a return train ticket to the city. I no longer remember the actual fare but for an eleven-year-old boy it was very little, certainly not enough to strain the resources in Dad's mulga wood bowl.

Probably my real transgression was going to the city without first asking for permission. Dad had been ill on and off for as long as I could remember. He slept a lot. Mum operated a small grocery shop in a separate brick building in front of our home. Her days were very full. If I slipped away for an hour or two it would hardly, if ever, be noticed. And if I had been asked where I was, 'just playing' was always an acceptable answer. I was, after all, a child in short pants, an innocent, what else would I be doing?

One of my addictive passions and most constant reasons to dip for change was to buy the pleasure of riding the rattling, red railway train into the city. From the Flinders Street station, Melbourne's iconic hub for all the trains, I would cross the street and walk through the archway by the Cathedral, past St. Paul's Chapter House, down some stairs, and into Regent Place. There at the end of that small arcade was my ultimate destination, my altar of worship, the retail façade of Tim the Toyman.

God would surely fail to smile upon any parent who had either willfully or carelessly neglected to enrich the life of his or her child with visits to that place of wonder.

I think it was a spring day but I can't be sure of that. I do know it was late afternoon on what had been a school day. I was in my school uniform of grey wool shorts, long grey socks and a grey blazer boldly sporting the blue and gold badge of St. Bernard's Christian Brothers College. And a cap! Oh, my goodness, one had to wear the cap. Students who were sighted on the streets not wearing their caps were publicly identified and humiliated in class and silently condemned to hell.

I stood there looking through the glass at the counters inside the shop where the true wonders were safely locked away. I didn't have pockets heavy with coins. There would be no time lost debating should I buy this or should I buy that. I wasn't there to buy. I was there to look. Having enough money to buy one of the toys never even crossed my mind. There was no reason to pine about it. It simply wasn't possible and I knew that. My pleasure, my honest joy, was just looking at the wondrous things Tim the Toyman had to offer.

The saleswomen were my friends. They had come to know me. They would never pressure me to buy something. They knew better. But they wouldn't hesitate to ask if I would like to see something up close.

There was one particular toy with which I was totally enthralled. I had looked at it in wonder more times than I could remember and on one memorable day it had been taken out of the display case for me to see and touch. My joy was immense. It was a dream fulfilled.

To many, it was just another plastic cow, a black and white plastic jersey cow. To me, it was so much more. I had personally milked a cow like that once. We understood each other. The true miracle of that particular plastic cow was that, if you gripped the udder and carefully turned it one half turn to the left, the udder could be removed from the body of the cow. There, inside and attached to the udder, was a rubber bladder. If you plunged the plastic teats on the udder into a glass of milk and squeezed the rubber bladder it would fill with milk. Next, you would carefully insert the udder back into the body of the cow and secure it with one half turn to the right. Then, and this was when the true magic began, if you stood the cow up on her four plastic feet and pumped the plastic tail, milk squirted out the teats. It was amazing.

I had never actually seen the whole thing happen but the saleswoman had carefully explained it all to me and she had shown me how the pieces all worked together. I was enthralled. Who could have even thought of something as astounding as that? One day, I thought, I would have a cow like that and I would amaze countless others when I pumped the cow's tail.

"He seems to like that one a lot," said the man in the pale grey suit near the counter. There was a smile in the voice. He was obviously amused at how enthralled the littlie boy in shorts was with the miracle cow.

"Yes," said the saleswoman. "He's in here all the time looking at it." She smiled at the man. "Can I help you, sir? Is there anything you would like to see?" She moved away to serve the man. I didn't know the time but I knew I would have to leave shortly to go home, help stock the shop, and do my homework.

The saleswoman returned, reached into the showcase, and took my cow. She was going to sell my cow to a stranger. I was aghast. I didn't know what to say, where to look. What would I do now?

The woman soon returned, this time with a paper bag, which she handed to me. I was very confused. "This is for you," she said.

"What was it?" I said.

She held out the bag for me to take. "It's your cow, your milking cow," she said.

How could that be true? I just saw her take the cow and sell it. I carefully opened the paper bag and there was my beloved jersey cow resting in the bottom of the bag, just like she said. The sales woman leaned forward and spoke softly. "The nice man there bought it for you," she said. I looked at the man in the pale grey suit by the counter. I said thank you so softly I'm not sure he heard me but he smiled, gently turned and walked away. I never knew his name but I have never forgotten him or his random act of kindness.

It was one of those remarkable, seminal moments that help shape a life. For a long time I wished I had known his name so that I could, perhaps, have thanked him more completely. But now, I have come to understand that he didn't need me to know his name. He didn't need praise nor attention. That wasn't why he bought me my cow. He just wanted to make someone happy and that was exactly what he had done. My surprise, my appreciation, and my joy were his reward.

There is a lesson there that I hope I have learned. If every now and then I can buy someone his or her own totally loved but totally unexpected plastic cow, then I have honoured the man at the counter in the pale grey suit.

Life on the Edge.

Discovering a richness of life at both ends of the journey.

I am in the city to see a friend. We haven't been as close in recent times, although we had enjoyed seeing each other when the chance arose. Whenever I think of her, I see her bright eyes and hear her laughter. Back in the dark ages, we had worked together. They were important times. We were all of a similar age and we were all forging our respective ways into life.

One of the things I admired about her most was her indomitable spirit. When she wanted to do something, see something, be somewhere, it happened. She and her partner travelled to the wonderful and exotic places most of us only talk about. She has taken thousands of photographs and has had numerous exhibitions of her work. When they weren't amassing travel points, they relished the city in which they lived. Galleries. Plays. Exhibitions. No moments were wasted. They did it all. So much so one could too easily forget that she had been living with cancer for an unreasonable portion of her life.

The patterns repeated themselves. The cancer would invade. She would endure the rigors of treatment and find remission. The cancer would retreat, regroup, and invade again. She would resist again. She would prevail again. That was the way it went for twenty-nine years.

Now, she has brain cancer. She is dying.

The speed with which she has gone from having a little difficulty finding words to facing death is staggering.

I know what a hospice is. I know what palliative care means. Or do I? These things I thought I knew were academic, detached. What I was facing now was real and it was clear that I had no real idea of what lay ahead.

When I first arrive at the entrance to the hospice, a young woman greets me just outside the door and explains that I would have to wait; there was a procession happening. "Of course," I say and step aside. At first, it didn't gel, I didn't quite know what she meant but it became clear almost immediately. How naïve I was. The procession is a funeral procession. A dozen mourners walk out of the hospice and look lost. Soon they are followed by a coffin, which is quietly transferred to a hearse and gone. Some hug. Some cry. Before long, they all drift away. Processions are not extraordinary here.

The same woman who had previously asked me to wait returns. She smiles and beckons me to enter. Another woman greets me and I think she asks if I am there to see someone. I don't know what to say. I stumble and stammer and finally make some sense. All the time I am wondering what I should be saying, what are the protocols when I just turn up unannounced? My disarray is clear but this is nothing she hasn't seen many, many times before. I am asked to sign in while one of the nurses says she will locate my friend for me. In contrast to my mild confusion, there is a pervasive sense of calm and order here.

This particular hospice has a long history of charity and care. It was originally built as a chapel and subsequently became a hospital in the late eighteen hundreds. As I walk from the reception area toward the back of the building, I pass through a Great Room, replete with high ceilings and stained glass windows. The furnishings are contemporary and subtle. There is a large seating area, rather like you would find at a lodge. As we continue deeper into the building we pass a long wooden dining table that flanks one side of an open kitchen.

This isn't anything like what I had expected. Oh, I know that not every hospice has the same ambiance and sense of history but I feel sure they all share the warmth of humanity that the staff and volunteers bring to it.

We are into the Fall season but the sun is still warm. The nurse smiles when she tells me that my friend and her partner are in the back garden, making the most of the bright day.

We reach the door leading to the garden and I pause to look through the glass window in the door. There they are as promised. She is in a bright chrome hospital bed on wheels. She is completely swaddled in soft blankets and crisp white sheets; all I can see of her is her face. Her partner, seated beside her, leans across her body, his head almost on the pillow beside her. It is so unlike how prime time television has conditioned us to believe death should be. There is no violence, angst or maudlin drama. This is simple, fragile and tender. I momentarily feel I shouldn't intrude.

This visit is a good one. She doesn't move, perhaps she can't. If she does speak it's quiet and brief. Putting the pieces together is not an easy task. The cancer hasn't won every bout, she can still laugh and smile and I shameless play to that. It's wonderful.

It seems that we have just relaxed and settled into the conventions of the day when a nurse arrives to take her back to her room. My friend has had a good day but that is it for now. She must rest. I know we are going to lose her and soon but despite what has been stolen from her she is very much alive today. I was lucky to share that time with them both.

Her partner travels with them back into the hospice. He has been relentless in his care and kindness. He is there every day beside here and will be there every day she needs him. I retreat to the Great Room to wait for him.

Death, however we rationalize the inevitability, is still shocking. It steals away part of our own lives every time we lose someone we hold dear. On this occasion, however, just knowing how richly she has lived and that she is now here, in a place where staff and dedicated volunteers work relentlessly to make every minute matter also helps ameliorate the loss.

There is dignity in this place. You are not just someone dying. You are someone.

I am sitting at the kitchen end or the Great Room. At the other end, in the lounge area is a family. I don't know these people but I find the subtle drama of the moment so compelling. Gathered around on sofas and armchairs are these people who have obviously have come to visit someone they hold dear. I have to remind myself where we in a hospice, a place people come to die. Yet, over there, there are no tears, no wringing of hands, no visceral angst. There is laughter. There is conversation. On the sofa are some boys whom I guess are in their late teens. There is a woman close to fifty and a man whom I think is the father. He's bright and engaged and despite the grave subplot, he's making the most of his time. Next to him is the one person they have all come to see.

The last thing you want to do at a time like this in a place like this is stare. I know that but I keep going back to him. I try to measure my attention. I calculatedly look away now and then. I monitor the family to see is anyone is monitoring me. There is something indecipherable about him. Simple, subtle things challenge me, like how old is he? Grave illness muddles everything. I decide he is relatively young, maybe a little more than thirty years of age. That alone is shocking, brutal, and unreasonable. Whatever ravages him is ruthless.

He can be there with them. He can listen. He can, on occasion, respond. But everything is muted, filtered through the real circumstance of where he is in life. This is a young man inexorably trapped inside a withering, fading body. His skin is grey, a flat, dull, grey. I have seen people ill. I have seen people die. I have never seen anyone bloodless. He sits slightly stooped; an intravenous line runs somewhere across his body. His hands are fine and delicate; he gestures little. His hair is a mat of short blonde stubble that likely bears witness to the ravages of chemotherapies and chemicals. If I visit the hospice again, he will not he here, of that I am certain.

There is a profound difference between looking at someone and saying "he doesn't look well," or "he seems to have failed a lot" or even "he is very, very ill". These are the polite euphemisms we use to insulate ourselves. They are of no use today. He is dying. We have lost him, dear soul. The measurement of time beyond today is meager and there will be no reprieve.

This is death sitting on the edge of life.

I don't think I will ever forget that young man and the people around him. One of the boys on the sofa laughs softly. Others around him smile and share the moment. Their life reminds me of the life that surrounds all of us here. This is a place where the path is eased for everyone, those who still live just a breath away and those who will live on without someone loved.

This is a house imbued with kindness where death is given dignity.

We should all do this well.

Better Left Unsaid.

Shopping for the essentials that held life together, like conversation, friendship, and a sense of community.

"Doesn't anyone care anymore?" Vera Brook was angry. A strong wind had blown newspapers into her front yard. To most people, that would be a minor annoyance. To Vera, it was a personal assault. Every sheet of paper snatched from the rose garden was waived in the air as if evidence of the conspiracy against her.

"Who threw this here? Come on, who did it?" Nobody looked out a window. Nobody came to her rescue. Everyone who lived on Margaret Street had grown accustomed to Vera's tirades.

Vera had spent her entire life in Moonee Ponds, an inner suburb of Melbourne that was bustling with growth in the 1950s. She was quiet, polite and a tad eccentric. She had a penchant for cats and taste for sweet sherry. She enjoyed her weekly forays to the shops on Puckle Street.

She loved to look in windows, sometimes try on a new dress, or visit the chemist shop to see if there was a perfume to sample. There was a warmth and familiarity to the place that comforted and reassured her.

Nobody could remember exactly when all that changed. Vera became increasingly withdrawn. Where her eyes once greeted on-comers, they were now downcast. "What's up with Vera?" a few would ask. "She was always a little odd," others would say and that was that. In more recent times the changes became impossible to casually dismiss. Given even the mildest provocation, she would proclaim the perfidy of life and how all who passed by were more or less damned.

Some who had known her in happier times were bravely tolerant and, at the very least, civil. Now, most people calculatedly looked the other way, crossed the street, or ducked into a shop if she approached.

Even Vito, who owned the greengrocer shop opposite the Moonee Ponds railway station had reached the end of his tether. Over time, Vito and Vera had developed a unique and oddly undemonstrative friendship. He would occasionally have too many fresh green peas so he would fill a paper bag with peas and set them aside for Vera. She would occasionally make too much stracciatella soup, Vito's favourite, so she would take glass jars of soup to Vito's shop and leave them beside the cash register. Neither would acknowledge true intentions. 'I had too many' or 'I made too much' always rationalized their actions.

Vera's disposition was particularly bleak as she stepped into Vito's shop one day in late summer. Vito was in a miserable state himself. Deliveries were late, produce was spoiled, he was nursing the aftermath of Chianti overload, and a small child who wanted to touch everything was shrieking. Nothing was going right for Vito. Nothing could be right for Vera.

"Look at that lettuce, it's stale," said Vera, a little too loudly.

"It's fresh!" said Vito. He had no patience for Vera on that day.

"It's rusty," said Vera. Vito waved his arms as if to completely dismiss her but Vera was not about to relent. "And those tomatoes."

"They're fresh!" Vito insisted. The unhappy child in the corner had notched up the level of his tantrum.

"They're soft!" shouted Vera, jabbing at them. The crying grew even louder. "For goodness sake!" Vera glared at the mother of the two-year-old who would not be placated. "Take the child outside if you can't control him," she snapped.

"What did you say?" Vito slammed a sack of potatoes to the ground and stormed over to confront Vera. "You don't talk to my customers like that!"

"I'm just saying...."

"No, you're not saying anything. You've said enough!" roared Vito. "What the hell is wrong with you?" Vito had never before spoken to her that way. Vera became very flushed and confused. She fidgeted with her purse and her pockets as if looking for an answer. Vito hovered over her, arms flailing wildly in the air. "I'm sick of your complaining, you hear me. All the time, that's all I hear any more I'm sick of it. Everyone's sick of it. I don't know who you are anymore."

Vera couldn't speak. She couldn't cry. She could barely breathe. She made a hasty retreat to the street and didn't look up until she had securely closed her front door behind her. She had been hurt. Deeply. And she sincerely regretted making Vito angry. She wished she could explain but knew she couldn't. It wasn't the child that upset her. It wasn't the freshness of tomatoes or the texture of the lettuce or the colour of the cauliflower. It was, quite simply, everything else in the world.

Despite the inevitable inconvenience she never went near her former greengrocer nor any of the Puckle Street shops again. From that day on, she vowed to buy all she needed from Molly Brennan's grocery shop on the corner of Smith and Margaret Streets. What she couldn't find there she would live without.

Molly's shop was a stout, little brick structure built around the turn of the century when this suburb of Melbourne was finding itself. The roof was grey slate and, even after all that time, was still in excellent condition. Floors and counters were solid wood and well scrubbed daily. A large window flushed the interior with natural light and the gold filigree work on the windows, although faded, still mustered distinction as it subtly boasted the favour of Bushell's tea. Going to Molly's corner store was hardly like shopping at all. It was like visiting a friend.

There was a wooden chair beside the counter and close to the window where you could sit and shop and chat about the large and small of life. One of Vera's favourite times to be there was first thing in the morning when fresh loaves of Procera bread were transferred from the wooden shelves inside the horse-drawn delivery cart to the wooden shelves that flanked the main counter of Molly's shop. The seductive aroma wafted through the shop and lingered for hours. Vera found immense comfort in the ceremony. The predictability and simplicity of the act fed her as richly as the bread itself. Sensual pleasures like that had become precious and rare. They were not to be hurried. She quietly sat and relished the moments.

"How's Paddy today?" she finally asked Molly.

"He's doing well thanks, Vera. He had a good night last night."

"How many heart attacks has he had now?"

"We're not actually keeping score, Vera." Molly really wasn't in the mood to revisit Paddy's heart attacks. "Can I get you anything?"

Molly's curt dismissal of the question made Vera anxious. She snapped open her black leather handbag and began to rummage through the contents. "I know I had a list," she said. She didn't have a list. She never had a list. Rummaging through the purse was a device that bought her time to find a response when she felt flustered or confused.

"Sugar. I need some sugar," she said a little defensively.

"Sugar? One or two pounds?"

"Just one pound. No, I think two pounds would be better. I'm thinking I might make some jam."

Molly fetched a two-pound bag of sugar from under the counter. "There you go." She placed the sugar in front of Vera. "Is there anything else?"

Vera couldn't think of anything else so she just shook her head. "I should get going, I have a lot to do, today." Vera reached for the sugar with her right hand, winced and dropped the bag onto the counter.

"What is it?" Molly watched Vera pull her right arm close to her body and clench it tightly.

"My arm's crook, real sore today."

She studied Vera for a moment and knew this was not a façade to garner sympathy; the woman was in real pain. Molly walked around the counter to where Vera sat. "Where does it bother you?" she asked and knelt before her. Vera had now firmly clasped her armpit. "Show me, Vera. Is it under your arm there? Is that where it hurts?"

"No, no, no, it's fine. Just noticed it now. Must have bumped it." Vera rose to her feet and stepped away from Molly. "Get one of the boys to drop the sugar off when they get home from school will you? I have to get going, can't sit here all day talking. I'll never get anything done."

"You must have that looked at, Vera." Molly insisted.

"There, that's for the sugar." Vera placed two shillings in Molly's hand.

"When are you due to see the doctor? I'll call him for you, shall I?

Vera hastily returned her purse and papers to her bag. "Wouldn't it be lovely if you could have fresh meat in the shop? Lean lamb chops would be nice." Molly handed Vera her change. "And maybe some sausages. Not skinny ones, nice plump pork sausages. I have to go now."

Molly reiterated the need to see the doctor. "Don't wait for an appointment, Vera, just go." Vera simply waved and headed home still holding her arm close to her body.

The next time Molly went to Palmer's Butcher Shop on Puckle Street she picked up two lamb chops and a pound of plump pork sausages and then dropped them off at Vera's Victorian cottage. It had become a ritual, the details of which were never actually discussed. Vera always left money on the dining room table. Molly would enter, the door always being unlocked. Vera would call out from the bedroom to enquire who was there. Molly would assure her not to worry and that she was just checking in. And that was that.

It was three years since Vera had her left breast removed. It had been a shocking and sudden assault that seemed without consideration or reason and it left her confused and angry. Stepping back into life had been a constant battle. For two years she privately prayed that her bitterness would abate and she would resolve some level of forgiveness for the world. Then, late on a grey Thursday afternoon, she discovered that all her resolution and effort was for naught. The monster was back. Almost precisely two years to the day after her surgery, the cancer had returned, this time invading other regions of her body. It was a cruel and savage betrayal.

At Molly's continued insistence Vera finally made an unscheduled visit to Dr. Egan's surgery. She sat on the hard vinyl seat doggedly waiting for the doctor to return from the hospital. She declined a glass of water. She declined a cup of tea. She was afraid that if she stood up her legs would carry her out the door, never to return.

When the door finally opened it wasn't the doctor who entered, but Vito; he had come to pick up a prescription. Vera immediately averted her gaze in the faint hope he wouldn't notice her. Ignoring him was the wrong thing to do. It was rude. She knew that but it was too late, when she looked up again he was gone.

Much to Vera's surprise, Vito returned just a few minutes later, this time with a paper bag in his hand. He hesitated for a moment and then crossed to where Vera sat. She looked up at him uncertain of how to respond. Vito smiled. Vera nodded. Vito nodded. "I got some lovely fresh peas in today," he said to Vera. "Real sweet they are."

"Oh, yes?" Vera's response was awkward, uncertain.

"Think I ordered too many, though."

"Oh."

"Right," said Vito. He placed the bag on the seat beside her. They nodded to each other once more and Vito went his way.

It was a good twenty minutes before Dr. Egan arrived. He was a gentle, affable man who genuinely cared about life and how it should be lived and shared. He arrived at his office exhausted from his rounds at the hospital. The nurse at the reception desk silently drew his attention to Vera,

"Hello, Vera. How are you today, dear?" Dr. Egan placed his bag on the desk and sat beside her. "I'm sorry if I kept you waiting, dear. Was I expecting you?"

"No," said Vera "I didn't make an appointment." It was more of a challenge than a statement. Dr. Egan was well acquainted with Vera's demons. He gently clasped her hand in his.

"That's all right. Let's go in and talk about it, shall we?" he said.

Vera nodded. Even though he was darkly complicit in her tragedy, Dr. Egan was still one of the few people she trusted. His genuine concern was a comfort to her and just perhaps, if redemption were to be found, it might be through the touch of this plump, bespectacled man. She clenched his hand a little more firmly and tried to stave off the tears that were welling in her eyes. "I'm sorry," she said.

"There, there, there, nothing to be sorry for."

Her eyes nervously darted around the room searching for some clue to help her find the voice she needed. "I'm afraid," she said.

"Of course, you are," he said, squeezing her hand a little tighter. "And do you know what frightens us most? It's what we don't know. That's the worst of it." He smiled gently as she struggled to regain her composure. "All right?"

Vera nodded. "Come with me and we'll talk about it," said Dr. Egan. He helped her to her feet. Vera reached back for her bag of peas and held them close to her breast. Dr. Egan led her across the smartly polished floor of the waiting room and into his office.

He never let go of her hand.

Three days later Molly stopped by with her delivery from the butcher shop. The house was silent except for the muffled sound of a distant voice.

"Vera?" Nothing. "Vera? Are you there?"

Molly tentatively opened the bedroom door. The room was cramped and dark. All the blinds had been drawn. A small, brown, Bakelite radio sat beside the bed crackling its report of the day's news.

Lying under the covers and looking at peace for the first time in years lay Vera. Her anger and disappointment had evaporated with her life.

Molly turned off the radio and quietly closed the door behind her. She gathered the parcel of meat and instinctively took it to the kitchen to stow it in the ice chest. The kitchen was untidy. A fry pan lay in the sink; used pots sat on the stove; eggshells littered the counter.

The air was unusually fragrant.

Vera hadn't ranted or fretted or cried on that afternoon before her nap.

Instead, she had chosen to make soup.

My Last Night.

It's just me and my dog against the night.

It wasn't extraordinary. It was just another night ending yet another day. I hadn't eaten anything exotic. No oysters teased with fois gras or duck fat. No truffle-stuffed boar. I think I had fish and chips for dinner although I really hungered for chicken wings. As for drinks, there were no tumblers of absinthe, just a sympathetic and very compliant New Zealand sauvignon blanc with which my body had become intensely familiar. That was it, one glass of wine. Okay, maybe two glasses and some scotch. I think the most frightening thing I saw on television that night was 'Say Yes to the Dress', so, why couldn't I sleep? My wife had been out of town for a few days. Nothing extraordinary there, it had happened many times over the last thirty something years. I couldn't feel lonely, not with Zoe, our schnoodle, all fluffy white and ink-eyed, waiting to spoon me.

One more game of Free Cell, one more check of the email to see if there was any breaking news that was actually both breaking and news and then it would be time to roll over and turn off the light. On any normal night, I would close my eyes and drift off to blissful sleep before a minute had elapsed. Why should that night have been any different? And yet it was. I just lay there, suspended in the silence of the room.

The dog snuffled and broke wind.

Lottery disbursements are my sheep. I have a penchant for briefly worrying about how to share my immense lottery winnings. I am enormously generous and I want to be sure I've taken care of everyone. Sometimes I also worry that if I do win the lottery I'll be too shocked to remember my complex philanthropy. More precious minutes that should have dissolved into sleep have flittered away and I could do nothing about it.

Zoe snuggled in a little tighter and snored.

We live in a country town. There were no distant sirens, no echoes of life thrashing in the streets below, just the peaceful, bucolic silence that people wrote about in centuries-old pastoral poems.

It was somewhere between fifteen minutes and three hours that I had lain there mentally drifting and fretting. What to do? What to do? What could I think of that would induce sleep? The obvious answer, my novel. That should do it. It had gestated for over five years and I was finally on the cusp of writing it down. I once thought the concept was brilliant. It had started life as a compelling tome that explored how achievement-based learning had shattered the lives of three close friends. Lately, though, that had all begun to feel less exciting to me. It had lost an edge. What if I were to write about something more immediate, I thought, something more compelling, more universally appealing? Something like chicken wings.

Winged Victories I could call it. No, that's too Greek. Wing Wars would work better. It's about chicken wings that have been genetically engineered so that the actual chicken is no longer needed. These wings fly free in huge, transparent, geodesic domes. They're harvested in nets and then shipped to chicken wing outlets around the world. 'No chickens were injured in the making of these wings'. Brilliant. They become a huge success. But now, the Dark Wings, a subversive strain spawned by overbreeding, is causing dissent and unrest among the good wings. Battles ensue. Production is halted. Stock markets stutter. Wing Wars threaten to take down governments in smaller, chicken-dependent nations. This could actually be a great novel. My mind is racing. No, wait, this shouldn't be a novel, this should be a movie. A big movie. Imax. Guillermo del Toro will direct. Yes. And we'll need a score. We'll get Bono? No, not Bono, he's too Spiderman. It should be, of course, it should be Bette Midler. Now I'm really excited. "For you are the wind beneath my...." Okay, that's it, now I've got to pee.

I was still humming when I got back to bed only to discover that the dog had encroached even further. It's a king size bed but I swear I would have had more room on a hospital gurney.

Sleep, dear God, let me sleep. There were no more idle thoughts about lotteries, cars, movies or Bette Midler. Oh no, now the thoughts had become more invasive, more relentlessly disturbing. I was immediately consumed by the one dreaded thought that has haunted all of us at least once at that certain time of life.

What would happen if I died alone tonight?

Yes, yes, yes, we're all going to die at some point, I understand that, but there is a vast, yawning chasm between 'at some point' and 'tonight'.

'At some point' reminds me of things to be done: I must find a way to stop those damn carpenter bees from boring holes into the fascia on the shed. I must try to remember where I put the key to the safety deposit box. The dog is due for her shots. Why didn't I ask the dermatologist about that rash?

'Tonight' is a totally different beast. Screw the carpenter bees. Who gives a crap about carpenter bees? I'm going to be lying here stiff and cold and nobody will even know or care. It will be three more days before my wife calls out "Hello, Darling, I'm home!" She will cock her head to one side and listen for a response. Of course, there won't be one and she'll think I've gone upstairs for a nap. This isn't a nap, damn it, I'm dead.

I had always thought of myself as being pretty useful. I took pride in that. But if I was dead, like totally dead, then I'd be pretty damn useless. I'd be a lump of meat on the turn between three-hundred-thread-count Egyptian cotton sheets. Oh, my God!

I rolled over to turn away from the hideous thought but it followed me. Zoe looked up with big moist eyes filled with wonder either saying, tell me what is bothering you my dear, kind, loving man or for God's sake settle, I'm trying to sleep. "Zoe", I said. She drew a little closer "Let's say it does happen. Let's say, God forbid, I do die tonight. Who will take care of you tomorrow? Huh? Who will feed you, brush you, walk you?" She could sense my angst. She studied me intently, as dogs do, and then licked me on the nose twice.

There it was, the sign, the way to do something useful before that dark cloud descended upon me. I immediately got out of bed, hurried downstairs and filled Zoe's water bowl to the brim.

When I hopped into back into bed I fell asleep almost immediately.

Neither of us died that night.

Pooja's Gift.

A story inspired by a wonderful, brave woman I once knew.

Nahan is a largely agricultural community situated on an isolated edge of the Shivalik Hills. There are numerous apple orchards, ginger farms and a very large peach plantation. Nahan is about two hundred and sixty-two kilometers from Delhi. This historic site is a popular attraction for tourists who like to explore the higher areas of Himachal Pradesh. Visitors discover a restoring sense of peace and freedom by hiking the many lush, undulating trails. Because the elevation moderates the heat, Nahan has a pleasant climate through most of the year. There are many Buddhist temples and monasteries to evidence the Tibetan culture that has become so well established there.

This was the home of Deepak and Suman Sharma and their daughter, Pooja. Deepak, a tailor, had lived in a small rented apartment in Delhi for two years before he had returned to his home in Nahan. He always longed to go back to Delhi. Deepak was not a happy man.

Suman was a pretty, slim woman who had a natural joy of life. Her formal education was sparse but she was naturally bright and a very attentive, devoted mother for Pooja. Her gentle, reassuring calm was a clear contrast to Deepak's anger.

One hot, humid day Suman returned from work in the fields and complained of severe headaches. She soon had a very high fever and then nausea, vomiting, and bleeding from her nose and gums. She had developed Dengue fever. Suman's case continued to deteriorate and her symptoms quickly progressed to massive bleeding shock and death.

Pooja was devastated by the loss. Deepak demonstrated appropriate remorse but saw this as his opportunity to move away. He bundled up their few, key possessions and he and Pooja were soon on the bus to Delhi.

Despite her unsettled home, Nahan had been a good place for Pooja. She'd had a small circle of friends and loved to take long walks and lose herself in the lush green areas around her. That relaxed bucolic life was quickly erased once they reached the city. Their new home was very small, crowded and seemingly lost in a clutter of dry and dusty streets. Clear air, soft shade and long folds of green couldn't have felt farther away.

Pooja's aunt Manisha, Deepak's sister, had always been fond of the girl and became determined to ease her niece's pain. She planned a surprise. For Pooja's tenth birthday she took her to Lodi Gardens. It was amazing.

Ninety acres of paths and fountains, tall trees and endless carpets of flowers. It was everything she had lost and more. That first trip turned her life around and Manisha knew it. It became a ritual that the two of them cherished. Every birthday, and on many occasions in between, Manisha would pack a lunch and they would catch a bus to the Gardens. Sometimes they stroll the gardens, watch the yoga or Pooja would just play with other children. The visits would always end the same way; after lunch Manisha and Pooja would sit on the grass by the big fountain and tell stories. Enchanting, simple stories that made Pooja laugh.

It was the days between life at Lodi Gardens that were the most telling. They were harsh and lonely. Over the years, her father became progressively bitter and withdrawn. Pooja vowed that one day she would get away and build a better, more balanced life for herself. When it was announced that she would marry and move to another continent, it was both fearful and exciting. At the very least it was an escape. Pooja hoped she would no longer be haunted by the past.

Toronto's Egan Park was a small park of about two acres named after an otherwise forgotten city councilor. He had fought to save a little green space in an inner suburb of the city that was in a rush to be gentrified. Although some progress had been made in balancing the transitions, lines were still very blurred between persistent poverty and fine pinot noir. The park had proven convenient for cutting off a corner and saving precious seconds for those heading to shops, restaurants or work. Although envisioned as an urban oasis, nobody seemed to have time to enjoy it that way. Everyone was in a hurry.

Pooja had first come to Egan Park when she was a new bride in a new land. It wasn't Lodi Gardens It was two acres not ninety, but it was green. It was a touchstone. She could sit on the grass, close her eyes, and pretend that clash of traffic wasn't really there beside her. This was her sanctuary from the life that surrounded it. It was somewhere she could trust on those days when she most needed to realign her life. This past week had been a difficult one.

She had been sitting on the grass behind a bench near the path for over two hours. It wasn't just the shade from the overhanging chestnut tree that dulled the image of her scarlet and ochre silk sari. Blood on her left shoulder has crusted; dirt from recent rains had muddied her hems. Strands of grey-flecked hair fell in straggled wisps around her thin face.

Today, she was not that girl giggling on the grass and telling stories.

Today, she was waste discarded on a lawn.

She never looked up.

Hours passed yet nobody noticed her. Or was it that people had elected not to really see her? How often as a society have we done that, looked away or crossed the street to avoid something that might be difficult? Is that a conscious choice? Or have we intuitively insulated ourselves from any harsh intrusions into the patterns of our own lives?

The woman with the cream Coach bag didn't even glance at her; she was busy texting to say she was running late for lattes with her witty and fabulous friends. The tall man in the blue suit hurried by to collect his car from service; he'd promised to pick up their son from soccer practice. The man with the black briefcase certainly saw her, he almost sat on the bench in front of her but he quickly moved on. The woman with the small dog stopped and looked at her but she didn't like Indian women, didn't trust them, and walked away.

And so time passed. And so Pooja sat there hoping she would die.

It was 3:25 in the afternoon of that fall day when Beth Lister, a teenage girl in a navy school uniform approached Pooja. She came close and just stood for the longest time just looking at her. "Are you all right?" she finally said.

Pooja looked up at the girl but didn't speak. The red veins that had burned into Pooja's eyes shocked the girl and she stepped back a little.

"What are you doing there?" said her mother from where she stood on the path. Beth turned to her but didn't know what to say. "Step away," said her mother.

"But she's been hurt," said the girl as she looked at Pooja, who had now cast her eyes back toward the ground.

"It's none of our business," said the Mrs. Lister. She was growing increasingly impatient with her daughter. "Right now, Beth. We're already late meeting your father you know that. Now, leave her alone, please!" The please was more of a command than a request. The girl was conflicted and paused long enough to test her mother but finally relented and left.

Pooja sank a little lower into the earth and attempted to pull her shawl more tightly around her shoulders.

It was less than five minutes before Beth and her mother returned. "We have to do something," said Beth. It was a clear challenge to her mother. "I told you, she's not well; we can't just leave her."

"Fine, all right," said her mother. She carefully stepped around the bench to where her daughter stood beside Pooja. "Are you all right?" she asked Pooja, already knowing that was a foolish question. Pooja failed to respond. "Can we help you?" asked the woman. Pooja looked up at her. The absence of life in her expression, the cruel deep bruise on her cheek and the dried saliva caked on the edge of Pooja's mouth shocked the mother. "Dear God," she said. "What's been done to you?"

She crouched down beside Pooja and took her hand. Pooja trembled but clasped the woman's hand in her own. Pooja gasped, sucking in the air. She didn't cry. Tears had been left behind a long time ago.

"Well, you can't stay here," said Mrs. Lister. "What are we going to do with you?" she said, directing the question more to her daughter than Pooja.

Beth had been busy on her phone. "There's a walk-in-clinic about two blocks from here," she said.

"That's it then," said her mother. "Give me a hand here." Beth crouched down and they started to lift the poor woman. Pooja shook her head. It was wrong. It was all so wrong but she couldn't resist the strength of the woman and her daughter who finally drew her to her feet.

Pooja waved her hand weakly in the air and struggled to speak. "Have to..." She couldn't finish the sentence. "Have to...go home."

"Go home?" said the mother. "Nonsense. You're coming with us now." Mrs. Lister had a strong sense of what had happened and allowing her to go home was completely out of the question.

Nothing was spoken as they walked slowly to the clinic. Nothing needed to be spoken when they got there, Beth had called ahead with the details.

When the nurse was about to pull the curtain for privacy, Pooja looked at Beth and her mother; she was afraid. "Don't you worry," said Mrs. Lister. "We're not going anywhere."

The doctor confirmed what the mother had feared to be true. Pooja had been beaten. They had discovered one broken collarbone and two broken ribs. There were contusions on her head, back and arms; her left breast was disproportionately swollen and discoloured. Old wounds had healed but still bore witness to years of physical abuse.

"I have to go home," said Pooja in a voice almost too weak to be heard.

"No, that's impossible," said Mrs. Lister.

"Please," said Pooja. "He will be upset."

"Well, he'll have to get over that," said the social worker who had been summoned by the doctor. "I'll speak to him for you," she said. "Is there anyone else I could call, do you have a son, a daughter?"

"Yes, no, my daughter...she's away."

"Okay, maybe we can reach her a little later but right now I need to take you to a shelter. Pooja, do you understand what I'm saying?" Despite Pooja's rooted instinct was to return to the source of the abuse, she was too overwhelmed to contest the issue.

There was no further discussion of the matter. Before Beth and her mother left the clinic, Beth placed into Pooja's hand, a small piece of paper on which she had written her name and address. Too weak to hold on to it, Pooja had let it slip away. Beth picked it up and put it in Pooja's hand again, this time folding her fingers tightly over it so she couldn't let it go.

Three months later, Beth received an unexpected letter. "It's from the woman in the park," she said. "She wants me to meet her there next week."

"I don't know," said her mother, "I'm not sure that's a good idea."

"You think ignoring her is a better idea?" said Beth.

"No, of course, you should see her if that's what she wants."

Beth paused at the entrance to the park. Pooja was sitting on the bench and not crouched behind it this time. She wore beige slacks, a blouse, and cardigan; closer inspection would reveal that everything was very clean but not quite the right fit. They had been donations but they looked well on her. She smiled as Beth approached and sat beside her. "Thank you," said Pooja.

Beth was pleased to see such a change in her. Pooja's eyes now glistened; her hair was held in place by a tortoiseshell barrette; scars and bruises had faded. "You look good," said Beth.

Pooja was unseasoned to compliments. She smiled and whispered a thank you. She gestured to her clothes. "Everything I wear, people just gave to the shelter. So generous."

"But no sari," said Beth.

"No," said Pooja. "Nobody had donated saris." She laughed a little. "Another time, perhaps. But for now this, this is the gift I have been given."

Pooja took a deep breath, reached into her bag and took out the piece of paper Beth had folded into her hand at the clinic. She held it up to acknowledge its worth and then restored it to the safety of her bag. "I wanted to say thank you for your dear kindness." Pooja reached back into her bag and took out a small package wrapped in tissue paper. "I made this for you," she said, handing it to Beth. "I hope you don't mind."

Beth tried not to rip the tissue that had been so neatly folded. Inside, was a small rag doll, barely more than six inches long. It was a woman in a sari, not of silk but of found cloth. The stitching was precise but the proportions were challenged. One leg was notably longer than the other. The head was a little too large for the body. It was obviously something Pooja had made by hand. "It's not very good, I'm afraid." Pooja was very aware of the doll's odd character. She studied Beth, anxious for reassurance that her gift was not considered silly or childish.

"No, it's beautiful," said Beth.

"I couldn't think of what else to give you. I used to make these for my daughter," she said. The landscapes between Pooja's emotions were very narrow and now her brilliant, deep eyes filled with tears. She blotted them away with a tissue and erased the more troubled memories with a cautious smile. She put the crumpled tissue back into her pocket and watched people pass by. "I am leaving soon," she said.

"Where are you going?" Beth was surprised.

Pooja couldn't answer clearly. "I don't know but I can't stay here." Pooja surveyed the small park one more time, taking in every detail. "I will miss this, all of it." A woman walked by pushing a stroller. A little girl was slouched over, fast asleep. "My daughter has gone away," said Pooja.

"What do you mean, gone away?" said Beth. "Where did she go?"

Pooja looked at her hands, she fussed with her wedding ring. It was clear she didn't have an answer. "Life became too difficult at home. I am hoping to find her." She stood and smoothed out her cardigan. "Thank you so much for coming. I must go."

Beth stood to face her. "But you don't know where you're going?'

Pooja's response was a gentle shrug and smile.

Beth felt frustrated that Pooja had come so far but the prospect of her wandering off without focus was frightening. "You worry me," she said.

Pooja gently raised her hand; a simple, gracious gesture that suspended the conversation. "I can work. I will be all right."

"You won't go back?" said Beth. "Promise me that."

Pooja shook her head. "No," she said. She pointed west. "My life is not there." She pointed east. "My life is out there." There was a quiet confidence in her gentle manner.

"Then you do know what you want?" said Beth.

Pooja nodded and smiled her gentle smile. She turned to leave.

"What is it, Pooja?" said Beth. "What is it you want?"

Pooja paused and considered that for a moment. She replied with surprising clarity and simplicity.

"I want to be happy."

She raised her hand, waved goodbye, and walked away.

The Big Night Out.

Some dates defy expectations.

It might have been more lust than love but I wanted to make a good impression.

I had asked everyone I could trust where I should take Monica for dinner. I wanted it to be cool but no so cool that I would look shallow and a slave to trends. Cool was probably the wrong word; I wanted it to be contemporary and interesting, even surprising. Bottom line, I wanted to make a good impression. It wasn't that I didn't get a lot of dates. At least, that's how I had rationalized it but the truth was that I didn't get a lot of dates.

I was a nice young man in my early twenties. That's what everybody said. "He's a nice young man." They didn't say I was charming, funny, bright, or a hunk, they said I was nice. I didn't harbour a lot of fantasies, I knew that I paddled in the edge waters of society but I also believed that could change. All it would take to boost my confidence would be constant courage and a few really good dates.

I had a friend from work, Trevor, who kept saying that his friend, Monica, was hot. He also implied she was easy. I had come to believe that when Trevor went to bed and lay face down on his mattress, every girl he had ever met, even at pedestrian crossings, was hot and easy. Trevor may have been boorish and immature but he had value; he made me look good.

One night a bunch of friends had gathered for beers; Monica was there. Despite Trevor's obscene nods and winks of assurance, Monica didn't seem in any way hot and easy. She was polite and pleasant. She was nice. What, I thought, did I have to lose? I took a very deep breath and asked her if she would like to go out on a date and to my shock and delight, she accepted.

This would be a good date. No, this would be an amazing date, I'd make sure of that. We would go out to dinner. Dinner is a great play for a first date. You get to sit and talk and get to know each other a little better and then when the food arrives you get to take a break and make pleasant noises.

Where to go was the big question. After extensive polling, Smak, loosely described as Scandinavian, fresh and unpretentious, won out as the current restaurant of choice. That was to be it then. I told Monica we were going to Smak and although she seemed a little puzzled, she said she was excited because she had heard good things about smirk. Okay, maybe she didn't know smirk from Smak but at least she feigned enthusiasm really well.

When we arrived at Smak on the big night, Anike, a Norse-like waitress with great teeth ushered us to a table for two. The table was of generous proportion but it rather sparse, as were all of Smak's tables. My first impression was that the place was a little Spartan. It was like we were having dinner in a Finnish sauna with the heat turned down. I felt sure that we'd be whipped with birch branches after dessert.

We studied the main courses earnestly. I felt a real tension that the food I ordered would be a reflection of me, the man. A truly neurotic fear and a clear commentary on my total lack of confidence. This was a first date and every choice I made confirmed or denied expectations. On the other hand, Monica didn't seem to feel the weight of the moment at all. She was delighted and relieved to see fish on the menu. "Oh, look," she said. "Fish. I do like fish. I think I'll order the fish." Feeling very satisfied with herself she folded the menu and placed it back on the table. "Are you going you have fish, too?" she asked. It would have been so easy for me to comply, but I felt the need to strike out on my own, to show that strength and independence I'd read about in a borrowed copy of Men's Health. I stroked my chin and looked over every item. Jackpot. There it was. Sweetbreads. You don't find sweetbreads on a lot of menus but they were something that my mother often served so there was a comforting familiarity and a yet a suggestion that I was a man who forged his own path in life. "I'm sure the fish is great," I said, "but I've always loved sweetbreads. Oh yes, it's sweetbreads for me!"

Monica seemed appropriately impressed. "I've never had sweetbreads," she said. "Would I like them? Should I order sweetbreads, too?"

"No," I said flaunting the breadth of my culinary experiences. "They're a slightly acquired taste. There is this texture thing. Probably safer for you to stick with the fish for tonight." I said. "If you like the look of my sweetbreads, I'll give you a taste." Monica warmed to that idea. So did I. I found the prospect of the sampling each other's food mildly arousing. I ordered wine, a dry and grassy Sauvignon blanc. Monica, again, was duly impressed. She didn't know the wine but loved the idea of trying something new; she hoped she wouldn't fall off her chair if she had a second glass. We both laughed at that.

Idle chatter, sips of wine and considered silences filled the time between orders being taken and food being placed in front of us.

"Here we go," said Anike. She flashed a brilliant smile as she arrived with dinner. She placed Monica's fish in front of her. It looked lovely. Soft buttery white with brown edges from the butter sauce; the accompanying green beans glistened; they looked crisp and delicious. I momentarily wished I had ordered the same thing. "And for you," said Anike, as she placed my dinner in front of me. She beamed at me, waiting for some sign of approval that was never going to happen. I didn't get that brave order of bland glands I had expected. Oh, no. Instead, I got two very large testicles on dry toast.

There was a look of shock and horror on Monica's face. She couldn't stop staring at my testicles. "This is....?" She had trouble finishing a sentence. "You ordered this?" She took her napkin off her lap and wiped her mouth to defend herself against any air that may have wafted over the offending body parts.

"Fish looks good," I said, trying to move the conversation to a safer place. It was all in vain. Monica had despaired of any salvation; she was dating a man with an unnatural affection for those things she couldn't mention. What would she tell her mother? She kept her eyes down and ate her fish in record time. Any brave efforts to rescue the moment with benign banter were in vain; the balance of the evening was tragically doomed.

The following day I called Monica a number of times and left a series of garbled messages. I felt certain that she had received my messages, even though she never returned my calls.

Now, almost a full year later, here I am planning a dinner of way more importance than the Smak fiasco or any of the other dubious moment in my last year's sadly distorted quest for romance. Serious lessons had been learned. I now knew so much more than I had known before. This next dinner would be a class event. It would not be anywhere that has a drive through. nor would it be a restaurant where you were asked if you'd like gravy with that. We would stay far, far away from Scandinavia and the scent of pickled herrings. This would be an evening that reeked of decadence and class. This would be French.

There was nowhere more French in town than The Dining Room. A luscious restaurant you would never expect to find outside the confines of the Marais. It was universally extolled for its culinary excellence and awful attitude. I had been told that they would evoke the true spirit of Paris and be rude to me all evening; they would even spit at me on the way out if I skimped on the tip. It sounded wonderful.

The real challenge with The Dining Room was simply securing a reservation. If you hadn't booked at least eight weeks in advance you had a marginally better chance of scooping a lottery win than you had of getting a table. Undaunted, I soldiered on. There could be no compromise. If that meant I had to grovel and debase myself to get what I wanted, I would do it. I knew it wouldn't be easy but I was ready for the sneering, the debasing sarcasm the utter disdain. I had stood facing the mirror in my bathroom for three nights saying terrible things to myself.

It was mid morning when I entered the restaurant, much too early for the lunch set to have arrived. Staff bustled around setting plates and glasses and cutlery with military precision. Some noticed me. Most ignored me. I was less than a spoon, I was nothing. It was everything I had hoped for.

Finally, the maitre d approached. He was a tall, streak of a man with a pencil moustache and a curled lip. I was sure I had seen him once before on a late night run of a 1950s French detective story. He looked at me for a moment and arched an eyebrow. "Yes?" he said.

I immediately felt I should apologize for being there but I repressed the urge. "I would like to make a reservation," I said.

"You would, would you? And for when did you hope to secure this reservation?"

"Thursday of next week," I replied with disarming confidence. He stiffened slightly and flicked pages in a big book. "Thursday of next week?" He found it quite amusing. He shook his head slightly to underscore the folly.

"Yes," I said, "Thursday of next week." It was time to play the big card. "I realize that it is short notice but it's a very important night. You see, that's is the night that I am proposing marriage and I can't think of anyway more perfect to do that than here."

It worked. I knew it would. He's French and there is nothing the French love more than brioche, cream sauces and romance. He paused and looked at the big book one more time. I was so anxious I wanted to pee.

'So," he said, suspending the tension. "Shall we say Thursday of next week at seven?"

Oh, my God. Touchdown! My heart did a fist pump. "Yes," I said with studied calm. "Thursday at seven would be excellent. Thank you - I'm sorry what was your name?"

"I am Jacques," said the maitre d, bowing ever so slightly.

"Thank you, Jacques, you've made...thank you, this means a lot."

"It's my pleasure," I said. "And what is the name of the very lucky person, may I ask?"

"Of course, I said. Her name is Janet,"

"Merveilleux," he said and smiled broadly, almost completely masking his disappointment that my fiancée wasn't to be Bruce or Chuck.

"Thank you again, Jacques." For a fleeting moment, I felt we had bonded. "Before I go could I please see a menu?" I said.

"Of course." Jacque handed me a menu, tastefully printed on parchment. Everything looked fabulous. The prices were equally fabulous. A plate of scallops cost just a fraction less than a small ocean-going trawler.

I studied the French descriptions of the dishes in detail. I try not be drawn to the small English translations below each item. Translations are always disappointment me, the true heart of the meaning is so often lost. It's like opera with subtitles. You want to weep for the tragedies that engulf poor Rodolfo only to glance at the subtitle and discover he's distraught because he burned his toast. I carefully worked my way through every item.

Jacques was becoming concerned. "Is there something in particular you're looking for? "

"No, no not really," I said, although that was not true.

"But you study it so carefully," said Jacques.

"Right, Well, I guess I'm just making sure, you know, that things are exactly what they seem to be." That didn't help Jacques in the least. "I don't want any surprises, that's all," I said.

"Surprises?" Jacques just looked at me. "I'm sorry I don't understand. You think there may be some, how can I say this, bad surprises with our food?"

"No, no, no," I replied. I had to say something better than that to allay his concerns. "Sometimes, Jacques, you know, sometimes you order something and you think you know what you've ordered but what you get is totally unlike anything you've ever ordered, or ever even hoped to order in your entire life. It's a surprise and not always a good one."

Jacques was now wondering why he had ever given me a reservation. I wanted to ask if he had ever ordered sweetbreads at Smak but felt that wouldn't move us forward. I needed to infuse the moment with a little clarity. "The thing is, Jacques, what it all comes down to is that I just needed to make sure there weren't any menu items here that could possibly turn out to be something else?"

"Something else?"

"Yes," I said.

"I don't understand," said Jacques. He was obviously losing patience.

"The surprise I mentioned, the bad surprise," I said.

"The surprise that you don't want to find?" said Jacques.

"Yes," I said.

"I see," said Jacques. "But what could it be, this bad surprise? You must tell me what it could be."

What could I do? What could I say? I had an immediate urge to point at my crotch but felt that could just take everything in another direction completely.

"What I was looking for? The thing I didn't want to find here was….."

"Yes?"

"Well…."

"Just say it." Jacques had had enough.

"Testicles," I said.

Jacque took a moment to consider all of this. "You didn't want to find…."

"No. Right"

"Are you saying you don't like…..?

"No, no, not at all. Never." I laughed nervously. Why I couldn't have just let it all go God knows, but I couldn't. I thought perhaps a little manly humour might save the day. "I mean I'm fond of my own of course. Very fond," I said. "But on a dinner plate? I don't think so." My false laugh slid into a higher pitch. I looked at Jacques; he was somewhere between appalled and aroused.

"I should go," I said. "Thank you, Jacques. Thursday it is then."

"At seven," said Jacques, still a little unsure of what had transpired.

I left The Dining Room without looking back. Next week would be the beginning of a new life with Janet and a fresh start for my nascent and confused relationship with Jacques. The world would be a better place again.

How did Thursday night come about so quickly? What does one wear when one is going to propose? You want to look really good, irresistible, whatever that means. I checked the closet and decided on a black suit. The black suit, the only suit I owned. I had bought a new shirt. It was white. Basic. Smart. Trustworthy. It would be all up to the accessories to add the flair. Do I go with the tie with the rocket on it, my personal favourite, the-don't-mess-with-me-I-mean-business tie, the really boring but safe tie I received for Christmas four years ago and never wore, or do I ditch the tie altogether and just unbutton the shirt? I went with the safe tie and immediately regretted the decision.

It was a late-summer night; the air was warm and embracing. I felt strangely calm as I walked to Janet's house. Maybe because I knew that what was about to happen was right, totally right. We had been dating for about six months and I knew this was what I wanted on day two. We had talked about marriage, children, all that. Mind you, it was all in very general, very non-specific, terms but she seemed to embrace the concepts.

I stopped at the base of the porch steps and checked that my tie was straight and my fly was zipped up. The restaurant, the flowers, the champagne, it would be brilliant. Janet had no idea how big this night was going to be.

I knocked on the door and waited patiently. Janet opened the door and smiled brightly. "Hi," she said. The greeting was right but everything else was wrong. She was wearing sweats. She never wore sweats on a date. Certainly not when she knew we were heading somewhere special.

"Hi," I said."Did you forget we're going out to dinner tonight?" She suddenly looked very vacant. I felt like I had kind of vanished from the porch. "Hello?" I said. "Big night. Dinner. Hey, I'm even wearing a suit." There was a smile again but not the sort of smile you expect from a loved one. It was more the smile you reserve for a shop assistant approaching the end of her shift. "Right," she said. It was just one word but it suggested that this brilliant evening was possibly in jeopardy. "Did you forget about this?" I said one more time.

She took an inordinately long time to answer my question. "No, not really," she said. Her eye darted nervously around and settled on the ground in front of me.

What did 'no, not really' mean? If she had forgotten that would have made me feel more than a little crushed. But if she hadn't actually forgotten and was standing there looking uncomfortable in sweatpants, then it was all just wildly confusing.

"Umm....," she said, finally.

"Yes?"

"Umm...do you remember I mentioned Robert?"

I nodded and grunted. What does he have to do with this, I thought.

"Well," she said and she pointed back into the house. "He...." She pointed back into the house again. "He's here."

"What? He's what? ? He's here?" I said in quiet disbelief.

"Yeah, he's here."

We stood staring at each other for what seemed like forty-five minutes. I mentally reviewed all the options. None of them were good. What there anything I could say to salvage the evening? He who was once he of the past tense was now present, very present, in both tense and person. That did not bode well. That did not bode well at all. It was suddenly all so fait d'complète. There wasn't much to discuss. "We're not going out to dinner tonight, are we?" I said.

"No," she said softly. "Sorry."

Sorry? Did she say sorry? I'd secured a table at The Dining Room, for God's sake. I told Jacques about my embarrassing bits. I have champagne on stand-by and all you have to say is sorry? Oh, I didn't mean to push that button and blow up China," said the President. "Sorry."

"I should, you know...go." She pointed back into the house again, back toward Bobby Boy, whom I had never actually met but now actually hated.

"Yeah," I said in a voice that said nothing. "You shouldn't keep him waiting." She smiled and looked away.

"Okay, then, one more thing," I said. "I'm just playing a crazy hunch here but I'm guessing there's no point in calling you tomorrow then, right?"

"Right," she said and for that moment I felt she really was sorry. "Bye," she said.

"Yeah. Bye."

Oh, my God. I've been dumped. I've been dumped on the doorstep on the very night I was going to propose. Man, how could I get all that so wrong? Walking down to her house, my life was a rapture of love and fantasy. I could see it all, that cute little house with shutters, a couple of pink-cheeked babies, and a dog, a brown lab. Pow! All blown out of the water, just like that. My whole life had become a lyric in a bad country song. I needed a drink.

I went to a social club downtown. I'd been there a number of times and I knew there would be friends who would smother me with love and sympathy and tell me what a fool she had been to let me slip away. That would be good. That would really help me. Unfortunately, that club met every other Thursday. The people on that Thursday night were total strangers and they all seemed to want to keep it that way. There was a girl who spoke French and asked me for directions. I helped her find her way. She was lovely and very grateful. I thought for a moment that I should ask her if she wanted to marry me or, at the very least, have trashy sex in the washroom, but I let it pass.

This wasn't where I needed to be.

Further down the street was a coffee shop. Cleo's. It was kind of an establishment. Everyone knew Cleo's except me, it seemed. There were three or four Cleo's around town and they had a cult-like following. It seemed like it might be a better fit. I could be less of a loser and kind of cool.

I sipped my coffee and looked out the window wondering if anyone who passed before me was having as much fun as me.

Laughter from behind me brought me back to the life in the coffee shop. I turned around to see about a dozen people at the counters. More precisely, there were a dozen guys in drag at the counters: fat guys, skinny guys, tall guys, short guys, all of them in high drag. One of them blew me a kiss and laughed. I wanted to shout "Don't any of you people know what happened to me tonight? A little respect, please!" Instead, I just smiled politely, finished my coffee and stood up to leave.

"Are you leaving, handsome?" said the guy who had blown me a kiss, which sadly was the nicest thing that had happened to me so far that night.

"Yeah," I said. "That's what I do."

The air had cooled and a breeze had picked up as I walked along the street back to my car. From behind me, I could hear the click of heels on cement. Just as I reached my car I turned to see who was approaching. It was a very tall, skinny guy in a red dress with matching spike heels. He looked a little pissed with the world. He stared at me as he grew closer. "What the 'expletive' are you looking at?" he said with a distinct lack of affection. I couldn't respond. I knew how he felt. I watched him walk away and hoped the night got better for him. It was when I turned back to the car that an old man lurched from a shadow and made a growling noise.

"Hey!" he said. "Hey there! Can...help me...huh?"

"I really doubt it" I replied.

"I've got to get to...shelter. I've got to...Salvation Army. Got to."

"You've got to what?" I just wanted to go home. I had the dregs of a bottle of cheap whisky. It had the tang and colour of horse urine but it was now very appealing.

"I got to.... you help me? Please, I got to...."

What does one do in a situation like that? Do you say, hey, go find a bench, or snuggle under a cardboard box, it's probably not going to rain tonight, but please just go away? Well, it was the first thing through my mind but I couldn't say something like that. I had a safe home, a warm bed, and bad Scotch. I was so far ahead of this old guy who leapt from the shadows. The easy response was to give him a few dollars and move on. He would be okay with that; it would, after all, fit the pattern of what had become his life. But then, as the night wore on, he'd need to find a box to lie under and it probably would rain.

"Where is this place, this shelter?" I said.

"What?" It was as if we spoke different languages.

"Where is the shelter?" I said. "Is it the one down King Street there? Is that the one?" I was now speaking much louder. Why do we think things will always be clearer if we shout? "Where do you want to go?" I asked him in a calmer, more reassuring tone.

He just stared at me. He couldn't find words. "Okay, what's your name?" I said. An equally difficult question, it seemed. He, poor man, was lost, deserted by civility, coherence, and comfort. His red-rimmed eyes were moist and glazed. His grubby grey-stubbled face was a hundred times creased. Even when he tried to smile, and he did try, there was a sadness overwhelming him.

I bundled him into the car. The Salvation Army Shelter on King was no more than ten minutes away but first, there was something else that had to be settled. We had to have dinner. My whole night had been designed around a dinner. It wouldn't be French. It wouldn't be romantic but, damn it, it would be dinner, and I deserved that. I was sure my new best friend hadn't seen knives, forks, and napkins for some time so we trolled through streets looking for a restaurant. We finally found one that was still open. It was pretty basic and they weren't too thrilled with my dinner date, but I waved money in the air and they made us food.

He relaxed a little and so did I. We almost maintained conversation. At one point we both laughed and I am still not sure why. He remembered his name. It was Joseph.

I don't think there will be huge changes in the texture of Joseph's life but that particular night had been a good one for him. He took my hand as we reached the door of the shelter. His grip was firm and steady. He kept shaking my hand as he struggled to find words. He wanted to say thank you.

I found the words for him and, in turn, thanked him for his company. I'm not sure he really understood. It didn't matter. It was a big night out after all. I'd had a date. He'd had a meal. And we were both the better for it.

An Inconvenient Child.

A true story of kindness delivered and kindness denied.

Helen held her glass of Chablis up to the light; she swirled the wine in the glass and watched ribbons of light ripple through it. She smiled. "Grant?"

" Yes?"

"You know what I'm thinking?"

"No even remotely," he said.

"I'm thinking that we should seriously start thinking about making babies."

"Oh, really?" The timing was a surprise but not necessarily the subject. It had been discussed and agreed that sometime down the road that could happen. "Should we finish our wine first?" he said.

"I'll be thirty-one, next year you'll be thirty-five. Sperm does have a best before date, you know. It's time we got married and made babies. "

"Well," said Grant. "You don't have to get married to make babies, you know."

"Are you trying to kill my mother?"

They vowed it would be a small wedding, family, and a few intimate friends; they would go to a nice restaurant for dinner after the ceremony. There were two hundred and thirty-five guests, and it was catered.

Right on schedule, they made a baby, a little boy whom they christened, Sean. He was to be the first of four children, or maybe three but definitely no less than two. Helen wanted a daughter, but that didn't happen. Instead, after a gap or almost four years, Billy was born to complete the family.

Grant and Helen were both busy with their careers, his in advertising, and hers in office administration. The constant shuffle and stress to see who could drop the boys at school, who could pick them up, and who could fill in for the babysitter who quit without notice were exhausting.

"We need a nanny," said Helen.

"We can't afford a nanny," said Grant. "We can barely afford to breathe. We shouldn't have bought this house."

"Rubbish," said Helen. "We needed a bigger house. The boys had to have their own rooms. We needed space for whenever parents come to visit."

They agreed that there was way too much stress, and a nanny would make life better for everyone. But how could they make that happen?

Grant was seated at a round table with four other people in a small conference room where they were earnestly discussing something less critical than world peace and only marginally more vital than the colour of dishwashing detergent.

Grant's secretary, Jane, opened the door, smiled at them and made the invisible phone sign to Grant. "Sorry," said Grant. "I have to take this."

"Fine," said a man in an expensive dress shirt. "But we have to get this resolved today."

"Absolutely," said Grant as he made his way to the door. "What?" he said to Jane.

"It's the third time Helen's called you." Grant sighed heavily and looked back at the meeting room. "I know, I know," said Jane. "She said it was urgent."

Grant took the phone. "Make it quick; I'm in a meeting."

"You've got time for this," said Helen. "Nanny. Did you hear that? Nanny."

"What the...?" He was momentarily caught off guard. "What are you talking about? What nanny?"

"Rose called me, no you don't know her, but she knows how desperate we are for help and she knows a place, an agency, that helps unwed mothers. She thinks they might be open to some kind of arrangement; we help them, they help us, that sort of thing. What do you think?"

"What do I think? I don't know. How old are these unwed mothers?"

"I don't know exactly. I can find out, okay?"

"Do you really want some messed up teenager in the house? We already have enough to deal with."

"She doesn't have to be messed up. That's a mean thing to say."

"They're young women, or more likely girls, who are pregnant and have had to turn to an agency for help. Think about it."

"Right, they need help. So do we."

"This is a terrible idea," he said.

"And you have a better idea? We have an appointment at two this afternoon with the woman who runs an agency. I can pick you up at one thirty."

"No," said Grant. "I can't do that. I can't just walk out whenever I want today; it doesn't work that way."

"And you think it's easy for me to get away? These people I work for, Grant, they're not missionaries, you know, they're accountants."

He glanced back at the boardroom and saw the expensive shirt looking back at him. "I can't. I'm in a meeting." There was a significant pause. "It's just impossible."

"I'm going on my own then," said Helen.

"Let me say it again; this is a terrible idea...." Too late, Helen was gone. He returned to his meeting, where they had decided to go back and review what hadn't been agreed upon so that they could move forward.

When Helen arrived at the agency, Evelyn, a thin, mature woman in a fitted blue suit, greeted her and ushered her into a small, informal, conference room. Evelyn talked at length about the girls, their circumstances, and their needs.

"I'm sorry to interrupt," said Helen. "I think what you are doing is wonderful, and I hope this doesn't sound selfish but what we're hoping for is some temporary support around the house, little things, you know, like keeping an eye on the boys," said Helen. "In return, we could offer her somewhere to stay until we can find a more permanent solution."

"Oh," said Evelyn. There was a momentary silence. "Of course, I understand completely," said Evelyn. "I'm sure we have some girls who are more than capable of helping out.

"I'm sure, but we were hoping, Grant and I, that we could find someone with a measure of maturity. More of a woman than a girl I guess I'm saying."

"We have had the more mature client, but you must understand, that's an exception, the norm is more like fourteen to nineteen years of age," said Evelyn. "But if, as you say, you're hoping to find someone who can repay your kindness by pitching in around the house, then I don't see any problem here. I hope I didn't mislead you when we spoke,"

"No, not at all." Helen knew this was an agency for girls even before she had arrived, but she figured that if she had at least pitched the desire of a mature candidate, then Grant would be more amenable to the outcome. "I just...my husband. I don't think he's as open to the idea." Helen was aware that there would be challenges, not the least of which would be getting Grant on board. "But I can't help but think what if I had a daughter and she...needed help, what would I do?" She glanced at Evelyn. "I'm sorry, I'm not quite sure what to say."

"Tell you what," said Evelyn. "Let's not rush into anything. I know we can find a solution here that will work for everyone but I think it would be wise to discuss this with your husband first, don't you agree?"

"Yes, absolutely," said Helen.

Evelyn flipped open her calendar and said that the coming Saturday at two would be good.

"For what?" said Helen.

"To bring Grant up to speed here. Help him become part of the process. I am sure he's a busy man and making time during the week can be so difficult for both of you, what with work and children. Saturday at two we said, didn't we?"

"Yes," said Helen.

"I am so glad you stopped by," said Evelyn.

"Saturday at two," said Helen. "Oh, my. Won't Grant be surprised? I can't wait to tell him."

"That's settled, then," said Evelyn. "Wonderful. Let me show you out."

Helen took a moment outside the agency just to breathe and convince herself that she hadn't promised anything specific. When she did tell Grant of the proposed meeting, he said it was a terrible idea. He was marginally relieved that no papers had been signed, no commitments had been made, but he was adamant that taking in a pregnant teenager was a terrible idea.

By Saturday the house had been spruced up, coffee perked, and a plate of very small sandwiches carefully arranged. The anticipated knock at the front door came right on cue at two. Helen opened the door; Grant stood slightly behind her, smiling but not meaning it.

His smile tightened when he discovered a cast of supporting players gathered behind Evelyn. They were a teenage girl and a middle-aged couple, all of who looked very out of place.

Helen heard Grant mutter, "What the...?" but being the ever-gracious hostess, she ushered everyone into the living room, just as if they had been expected. Evelyn and Helen exchanged the pleasantries of what a lovely house it was, how much cooler it has been, et cetera. The unexpected guests remained mute and detached. Grant had become obsessed with the presence of a small suitcase.

An awkward silence descended over the room until Evelyn took charge and handled the introductions.

"Grant, Helen, I'd like you to meet the Walters family." She gestured to the people behind her who had been seated on the sofa by the window. "Jim and Enid, meet Grant and Helen Maxwell, who have been gracious enough to have us here today. Enid was a short, stout barrel of a woman who nodded a lot. Jim was a slightly stooped man wearing a John Deere cap. He wasn't one for engaging eye contact. And here...." She gestured toward the shy, teenage girl seated in a chair beside the sofa. "This is Cheryl." Cheryl didn't look a day over fifteen; she couldn't lift her gaze from the floor. Evelyn was not about to let that social infraction pass. "Cheryl, say hello to Mr. and Mrs. Maxwell." She did look up marginally, and her lips did move as if to form a word. As lean an offering as it had been, Evelyn gave it a pass.

"Lovely, lovely," said Helen, buying time for more intelligent thought. "Coffee. Would anyone like coffee? I know I would. Let me fetch that for you." She rose and started her retreat to the kitchen.

"Let me help you with that, dear," said Grant, in hot pursuit.

"No, it's fine, dear, I can manage."

"No, no, no, what sort of a husband would I be?" He smiled at the guests he never wanted and disappeared into the kitchen.

"What the hell?" said Grant to Helen in a studied whisper. "Who are these people?"

"I don't know," said Helen. "Don't you start on me. If you'd come with me to the meeting...."

"So it's my fault," said Grant. "Great. There is a child in our living room, and she has a suitcase. Hello? Did you see the suitcase? I don't like the suitcase." Helen tried to ignore him and rearranged some of the sandwiches. "Did you at any point agree or even vaguely infer that we would even consider taking in this girl?"

"Of course not!" said Helen. He wasn't convinced. "What did you say to this women?" Helen stopped fussing and looked directly at Grant. "I don't actually remember now."

"Oh, my God," said Grant. "We are screwed. That girl is pregnant, right?"

"You don't know that for sure."

"The suitcase!" said Grant.

"Not now," said Helen. She handed him the large tray with coffee pot, cups, and saucers; she took the plate of sandwiches. "Be nice," she hissed as they re-entered the living room.

"Here we are," said Helen. "Now, who would like coffee?" Everyone accepted coffee except Cheryl. Helen asked her if there was something else she would like to drink; Cheryl shook her head.

The longer they sat there smiling and making small talk, merely confirmed Grant's supposition that these people didn't plan to take either the suitcase or their daughter with them when they left.

"Enid, why don't you tell us a little about the family and life at home," said Evelyn. Enid said she would love to, but she skipped over life at home, feeling it was more important to reassure Grant and Helen that both she and her cap-toting husband were very good friends with Jesus. They spoke to him pretty much every day. They loved Jesus. Both of them did. Loved him. They assured Grant and Helen that they would be talking to Jesus that very evening and would tell him of their kindness, and she wasn't talking about the coffee and sandwiches. She never actually mouthed the words but with every breath, she made it increasingly clear that this girl's careless impregnation could not be tolerated in any small town where parents conversed directly with Jesus.

A telling comment on the family dynamic was that Enid didn't speak to her daughter at any time during her sermon. Nor did she hold her hand, touch her cheek, or exhibit any physical affection. She did, however, take the time to reassure Grant and Helen that Cheryl was a good girl who neither randomly lit fires in basements, nor peddled drugs in schoolyards, nor owned a gun.

Grant had become certain that Enid and Jim's affection for Jesus would not have been reciprocated. He rose and smiled at everyone. "Would you excuse us for a moment. There are a couple of things we have to attend to in the kitchen. Helen?"

"Yes, the kitchen," she said.

They didn't speak at first; they just looked at each other. "If we're quick," said Grant, "we could make a run for it through the back door. They could find their own way out."

Helen felt she had to do something. She ran a tap. They both watched the water swirl in the sink. Grant reached over and turned it off.

"We have to do it," said Helen. There was a calm reassurance to her statement. "We have to take her."

"Oh, my God," said Grant.

"What's going to happen to her if we don't? Think about it!"

"I don't know, Helen! Why don't you ask Enid to check with Jesus, see if he has any better options?"

"Stop it," said Helen. "We can't leave her with those people, Grant; we have to take her."

Grant sighed and shook his head. "I know, I know." He took her hand. "Congratulations, you always wanted a daughter. Now, you've got one." Helen looked stunned and then let out a nervous laugh. "You do realize, don't you, that this isn't just a few days of benevolent inconvenience?"

"Oh, I know," said Helen.

"We're in for six or seven months of cohabitation with a girl for whom puberty is still a relatively recent phenomenon."

Helen didn't know whether to laugh or cry. They just looked at each other. There was some agreement between them, but before any final decision could be confirmed, they had to speak with their sons. They summoned the boys to the kitchen and asked them how they would feel about what had evolved in the living room. "No problem," said Sean, the older brother. "We'll take care of her."

"Can we go now," said Billy as he held up a bat, ball and catcher's mitt.

"Do you realize what we're asking you?" said Helen.

"Yes," said Sean. "You're asking if she can move in for a while, that we'll help take care of her, right?"

"Well, yes, right," said Grant. 'This is a big deal here, boys" he said.

"No, it's not," said the boys.

"Can we go now?" asked Billy.

"Yes," said Helen. The boys scurried out the back door.

"This is a big deal, why don't they see that?" said Grant.

Helen shrugged. "They're young," she said

"And we're old and jaded?" said Grant.

"Something like that," said Helen. "Who gets to tell them?

"You can be the hero," said Grant. "You tell them."

Evelyn was positively buoyant, and the parents were clearly relieved that they wouldn't have to take the little slut back with them. If Jim had had a gun with him right then, he would have fired it. The farewells between parents and child were perfunctory at best. They left Cheryl with more warnings than warmth; how she had to learn to behave, do as she was told, show respect, and so on and so on. Sentiments like they loved her, supported her and would miss her terribly never came up.

All of the dramas, the impending baby, the rejection by parents, the destruction of self-worth, all these things had happened a few years before the internet totally reshaped life. For Cheryl, there was no texting, no email, no

FaceTime, to link her with friends. There was a phone. That was it. A basic, uncomplicated touchtone phone. And the paucity of times that it was used told its own story.

Seeing Cheryl beside Sean and Billy was a study in contrasts. The boys were four to ten years younger than Cheryl, but it was far more than age that separated them. The boys had been raised in a creative, urban environment and had been lucky enough to travel to other countries and other cultures. Cheryl was from a small and relatively isolated country town. She was born and educated there. It wasn't just the centre of her life; it was the whole of her life.

The boys liked Cheryl. There was no posturing, no pretense. She was direct and honest. There was an initial resistance to involving herself in the day-to-day family operations, but that soon changed.

Cheryl grew very fond of Billy; a bond developed between them. He was still young, trusting and endearing but what mattered most of all to Cheryl was that he never judged her. She willingly agreed to walk Billy to school in the morning and then walk him back home in the afternoon. She had come to look forward to it.

Helen was cleaning up in the kitchen when Sean approached her. "Where is everyone?" he said.

"Well, your father is out for a bit, and Cheryl and Billy are in the yard. Why?" Sean looked reluctant to talk but stayed beside her and shuffled his feet. "What's up?" said Helen.

"It's Cheryl," said Sean. "I want to be able to talk to her, but I don't know what to say."

"Why? What's the problem?"

"I just don't understand. Why's she giving up her baby? I mean, how can she do that, just give it up? I don't get it."

Helen paused for a moment. Should she sit him down and attempt to explain all the ramifications? Or should she keep doing her chores and pretend it's not a big deal?" She settled on a position somewhere in the middle.

"I don't know when she made that decision, Sean, or why. But you have to remember that she is just a few years older than you. Are you ready to become a father?"

Sean thought that was a funny question. He laughed a little. "No,' he said.

"Right," said Helen. "Maybe she just doesn't feel ready to become a mother. Okay? It could be as simple as that." Sean nodded and accepted the response. "What we have to do is make her feel at home so that if she wants to talk about things like that she knows she can. No pressure."

"Okay," said the boy.

"Why don't you see what they're up to out there?" Sean started to leave. "And Sean..." He turned back to his mother. "That was a good question, son." It was a very good question. Helen had often wondered if the question had ever been discussed or was adoption just the assumed outcome?

It was Billy who had alerted his parents to Cheryl's impending birthday. The day she turned sixteen wasn't about to change anything in her life, but it couldn't be ignored. Helen made a dinner that focused more on fun than nutrition, and she baked Cheryl a birthday cake replete with lashing of icing, whipped cream, and sixteen candles. The boys made birthday cards and presented her with small presents that they had wrapped earlier in the day. She loved it, all of it. Cheryl was neither pretty nor plain, but when she did smile, which had started to happen a little more often, it switched on a light inside her. The only thing missing was a phone call, some proof that it wasn't just the temporary people in her life who cared.

Helen and Grant had retreated to the front porch with their glasses of wine. Looking through the window and back into the house they could see Cheryl and the boys were playing a board game she had been given. There was laughter.

"She's a nice kid," said Helen.

"Yes, she is," said Grant. "I'm sure Jesus must be bummed out by her slack parents." He put his arm around Helen's should. "No wonder the poor kid got pregnant," he said. "She wasn't going to find love at home."

The more time Helen had to talk with Cheryl, the clearer it became that the poor girl was totally clueless about the implications of her condition. Yet, it didn't seem to threaten her; some level of comprehension would have been necessary for that to happen. Helen concluded that her apparent ignorance wasn't an accident; it was her wall, her insulation from reality and she was less than keen to change that.

The Maxwell's role, as dutifully explained by Evelyn, was not to nudge or judge but to provide a comfortable and secure environment for her journey, and that was all. However, allowing Cheryl to pull the blankets over her head wasn't, in the minds of Grant and Helen, a prescribed part of the deal.

Time was no longer on anybody's side; Cheryl was a scant six weeks from delivery and despite her intransigence, Helen's persistence paid off, Cheryl finally agreed to attend birthing classes.

When the Maxwells initially heard that some of Cheryl's friends were coming to visit, they were pleased. It could only be good for her spirits. That's what they had hoped anyway. As luck would have it, these so-called friends turned out to be less than convivial. They came by the house but refused to come in. Grant and Helen smiled a lot and reminded each other not to make judgments. It was just after noon when her pack of erstwhile friends took Cheryl to a mall. Five hours later she called to see if someone could pick her up. Her people had become bored or distracted or both and had deserted her. It was rude and it was hurtful, but the real damage they inflicted was in the way they had successfully cajoled or bullied her into refusing to take birthing classes. It made absolutely no sense but these ignorant, rude people held sufficient sway over Cheryl to completely change her attitude toward education. It just wasn't going to happen. Period.

Besides, she knew exactly what lay ahead, or so she said. She'd seen it all on television. Her friends had seen it, too. Some movie where the girl with a gorgeous complexion expressed a moment of discomfort, pushed kind of hard twice, and extruded an adorable, albeit slightly mature baby that was a tad smaller than a Thanksgiving turkey. That's how birthing happens, and she knew it was true because she'd seen it on television. Hey, that girl in the movie didn't even muss her hair and two days later she went to the prom with that square-jawed quarterback. She sure didn't waste time taking no dumb classes.

There is a real caution here: when you know next to nothing, turning to people who know absolutely nothing rarely works out well.

Helen and Grant may have become concerned, but Cheryl certainly wasn't. At around 4:00 a.m. eight days later everything changed; her water broke. Toss in a few serious contractions and panic ensued. Helen had repeatedly explained to her how all this would evolve but, although Cheryl may have nodded to indicate comprehension, the reality had never landed.

Here was a child who was about to about to have a child. Grant called her parents. He let them know exactly what was happening and reassured them that their daughter was doing well but was afraid and needed them. He assured them that he and Helen would take Cheryl to the hospital and then he gave them clear directions and established a time when they could meet there.

Why had he bothered? He never really believed that they would come and, sadly, they didn't fail to disappoint him. It was Enid who explained how they would like to be there, but the timing was unfortunate or inconvenient or something. Jim's truck had to go in for service that morning; and there was a host of other pressing commitments: washing a dog, unclogging a sink, mending a fence, a litany of issues all far more critical than the birth of a grandchild. Grant was too angry to speak and hung up.

The ride to the hospital was tense, and it wasn't just Grant pushing speed limits. Cheryl was very vocal and utterly terrified to be on her own; she had clung to Helen's hand from the moment they left the house. When they got to the hospital, Grant opened the door to help her out, but Cheryl's knees buckled under her. Grant sat her back in the car and rushed into the entrance of the hospital where found a wheelchair. "Call me," he said as Helen pushed Cheryl down a hospital corridor.

It was over eight hours before Helen did find a chance to call. It had not been an easy delivery. It was just after 2:00 p.m. when Cheryl held her a seven-pound, five-ounce boy in her arms. Both were crying. Both were well.

Grant knew he should call her parents. Not out of any care or concern for them but because he knew Cheryl would want him to. And so he called. They answered. He delivered the news. There was no real joy at the other end of the phone, no sense of celebration. They were glad it was over, and that was that. Their shocking detachment was utterly consistent.

With what Cheryl had just been through, Helen felt she needed a few days to rest and recover. Not to mention her need to resolve the dilemma of her little boy: should she keep him or should she place him up for adoption? The next few days would be tough ones, and Helen felt Cheryl had a better chance of surviving the passage with them than she would have at what could only loosely be called home.

It would still be torturous. The transition would have been eased if there had been any rational discussion and agreement resolved ahead of time. Sadly, there never was any considerate conversation. She was bluntly told that the baby would be adopted, and that was that.

It was abundantly clear that her parents hadn't gone to the trouble of shunting her out of town only to have her return with a bundle of shame in her arms. Cheryl didn't contest that decision; she didn't know she could. All of that, of course, took place well before she had held her baby in her arms. He was utterly perfect. He was life. He had formed inside her, and she could feel the warmth of his tiny body nestled against her breast. Forget any previous plans and dictates; she didn't want to let him go. This was a crisis she hadn't dared even to imagine. There were many tears. There was much confusion.

A counsellor from the hospital arrived. She was a mature woman who appeared gentle by nature but clearly in control. "Hello, Cheryl, I'm Alice," she said. She held up a file she was carrying. "A couple of things we need to talk about, dear. Just take a minute or two," She turned to Helen. "You must be tired," she said. "Why don't you take a break while I chat with Cheryl."

Helen didn't need any further prompting. She needed to get out of the room even for a few minutes. As she sat in the small waiting room, she noticed a woman close by; it appeared she had been crying. "Are you alright," asked Helen.

"Oh yes," said the woman. "Thank you, though." She smiled. "I'm here with my daughter. She just had a little girl."

"That's wonderful," said Helen.

"I feel blessed that I could be here with her," said the woman. "Our first grandchild."

"That's very special," said Helen. "What is your daughter going to call her or is it too early to know that?"

The woman paused and considered the question. "Well, the thing is, the little one is bring put up for adoption."

Helen was shocked. "Oh," was all she could say.

The woman sensed some disappointment in Helen's voice and wanted to dispel any feelings of that kind. "It's fine, it really is. Anna's only seventeen; she wants to go to university, travel and educate herself to the world. She's just too young to be a mother. We talked about it a lot and every time we came to the same conclusion: this was best for both her and the baby." She took a moment to consider what she had just said. "It's not easy, but it's right. I got to be here with my daughter. We held hands, we cried together, and we could celebrate the birth together."

Helen could only think this is how it should be. You hold your daughter, you love your daughter, her life is your life. You don't send her away; you embrace her.

"Is everything good?" asked the women as she glanced back toward the rooms down the hall.

"Yes, it's fine," said Helen. She couldn't say how different life was for the two girls but felt she had to say something. "This isn't my daughter," she said. "Her parents are away; I'm just pinch hitting."

The woman could sense that there was a lot more to the story than was being told. "Good for you," she said. "I should go back and see how Anna is doing. We were giving her a little time with the baby."

"Of course."

Helen let her leave and waited for a minute before she returned to Cheryl and the counsellor. She was touched by the love shared down the hall and angry that Cheryl would never know that. It seemed so unfair.

"Ah, good timing," said Alice as Helen entered the room. "We're going to keep Cheryl here with us tonight. I think she'll be fine to leave tomorrow; you can check with the nurse in the morning to get an idea what time she'll be discharged. Cheryl and I agreed that we're going to hold off on completing the paperwork for a few days. Give her a chance to think things through thoroughly. In the meantime, the little one will stay with us, here in the nursery." She paused at the door and looked back. "You both look like you could use a good night's sleep. Good night."

Cheryl stared at the ceiling for a little while and then closed her eyes. Helen took her hand. "Are you alright? I should head home but if you need me to stay..."

Cheryl shook her head. She was physically and mentally exhausted. "Thank you," she whispered as she let go of Helen's hand.

"Good night, dear," said Helen.

When it came time for Cheryl to be discharged from the hospital, her parents couldn't be there. There was the predictable string of banal excuses, but they promised that they would arrive the following day. It was too much for Helen who picked up the phone. "Hello, Enid, it's Helen here. Grant tells me you can't make it down here today."

"No, I tried to explain to him...." said Enid

"No, no, please spare me that," said Helen. "You said you would be here tomorrow."

"That's right."

"Well, don't bother. We don't want you here tomorrow. In fact, we don't want you here for a few days. Let's say noon on the twenty-fourth. That's not negotiable, Enid. If you don't turn up, you'll be reported to the authorities. Goodbye." She didn't know which authorities she could call, but that didn't matter, it sounded good, and she could tell it shocked Enid.

At just after two the following afternoon Grant and Helen picked up Cheryl and took her home. Very little was spoken. No matter what they felt, their sentiments had to be muted. That was part of the agreement. All Grant and Helen could do was suggest without prejudice that she should think about what life would be like for her and her son if she kept him and, conversely, how would life evolve for each of them if her baby was put up for adoption.

Cheryl was so innocent, so immature, that life as a mother would unquestionably be fraught with all manner of frustrations. There was no father anywhere in the picture. When asked about the father, Cheryl couldn't be sure who it was. The subject was never mentioned again.

Giving birth had been the most vivid and compelling moment of her life. Through the clutter of confusion there was one fact that was bitterly clear: should Cheryl return home with a baby in her arms, the little boy would not be welcomed into a loving family. In Cheryl's heart, she knew that to be true, but how could anyone say to her that the best choice for both of them was to walk away. Cheryl felt physical pain as she struggled with the decision. She talked. They listened. She cried. They held her. She talked some more. Then, unexpectedly, she lapsed into a silence that lasted for a full day.

When she broke the silence, it was to call her parents. The conversation was disarmingly brief. The only question asked by Cheryl was when were they coming to pick her up. Her mother mentioned something about noon on the twenty-fourth. Cheryl said, no, not the twenty-fourth, tomorrow. They had to come tomorrow. She was firm about that. She couldn't endure the agony, and she knew that setting a hard deadline would force her to make a decision.

When her parents did arrive the following day, Helen took a moment to meet them outside the house. All they said was that they had come to pick up Cheryl. There was no small talk about weather or traffic, nor were there any words of appreciation, like thank you. That was fine with Helen; she had made up her mind to be dignified and restrained, but she didn't quite make it. She felt someone has to tell these people how utterly deplorable they had been. She told them they were terrible parents. She also mentioned that they were callous, unkind, selfish, and cruel. She didn't broach the subject of how disappointed Jesus must have been with them because she felt that was too obvious to even mention. They didn't protest. They didn't take a swipe at her. They just took it.

Before Cheryl got in the car, she handed Helen an envelope. "Can you give this to Alice, the lady at the hospital, for me, please," said Cheryl.

"Of course," said Helen. On the face of the envelope, hand printed in simple letters was its intention. "For my baby." Helen promised that she would take the letter straight to the hospital that afternoon.

When the car pulled away, Cheryl looked back at Grant and Helen and waved. As difficult as the concept of adoption had been, the final decision wasn't made to placate others. It was made because Cheryl knew that, under the prevailing circumstances, it was the right thing to do. It was her decision and hers alone, and there was some peace to be found in that.

Over the next few years, Cheryl kept in touch. She sent cards and the occasional photo. They had never spoken until the day she came to visit. She was nineteen years old and four months pregnant. She introduced them to Jonathan, the young man she was going to marry. She showed them a photo of the house they had rented in a small town far from Cheryl's parents. They seemed very happy together and were genuinely looking forward to the baby. This was not the naïve, innocent girl who had shared their home. She had matured in the past few years.

Jonathan stayed close to Cheryl the whole time. He seemed gentle and kind. He held her hand. He made her laugh.

Kindness needed and denied can leave a scar that often takes far too long to heal, if it ever does. Seeing Cheryl with her young man in one hand and a picture of her new home in the other was reassuring. There would be challenges no doubt, but it seemed that their Cheryl was going to be okay.

Sur La Plage.

A tale of toes, tattoos and clothing options.

It was time to escape. Off to St. Martin we go, that quirky, bicultural island in the Caribbean. Dutch on the bottom and French on the top. Choose your favourite flavor. We like the French side, and so our destination of choice is Orient Beach. It's far from our first trip there; we know the place well.

The familiarity fosters a sense of comfort and belonging. I know where things are. Walk downstairs and turn left. A smile, a bonjour and a buck will get you a fresh baguette almost any time of day. Think about it. Warm, crusty bread, a little French demi-sel butter, cream cheese, some black currant jam, and aromatic coffee, plus you can hear the waves a mere fifty meters away. It doesn't get much better than that.

Wine at breakfast doesn't generally happen before week three.

And what better motivation could there be to brush up on your French? I am actually pretty good with basic pleasantries like good morning, good evening, how are you, how much is the sauvignon blanc, and I'd like the gorgonzola pizza to go, please. The problem is that once you dash off these bon mots with panache, people assume that you are pretty damn proficient and off they go telling you about the son who disappointed them, the odd noise in their scooter, or the lack of prime time porn on cable. These are, of course, approximate translations as they go at such a clip I only catch snippets here and there.

My favourite thing to do on Orient Beach is walk. Well, that's the truth on any beach I guess, but Orient Beach ranks near or at the top of the list. A return trip is about 4.2 kilometers (2.64 miles), which I find ideal. One day in the middle of the first week of this trip I clocked up more than twenty-three kilometers walking, which is just over fourteen miles. I love it. My email was flooded with bravos and badges from Fitbit, my trusty fitness tracker. I slacked off the next days and barely make it over seventeen kilometers. Like I said, walking Orient Beach is my very favourite things to do. It even ranks above nude happy hour at the Perch Bar on the south end of the beach. Wait, let me consider that for a minute. Yes, walking wins. The south end of Orient Beach is Club Orient, a large clothing optional naturist resort. If you need to find me on the beach one day, you might start looking there.

Yesterday, I was up early and on the beach before seven in the morning. There is a wonderful sense of potential in the day when its shafts of early light leave long shadows across the wide swaths of sand. I find almost cultish the dedication among the true early birds who are there every day performing their ritualized promenades, some wearing shorts, some wearing nothing more than looks of contentment. It's only in the early hour of the day that one has that satisfying choice.

I had done the north end, which is always a good experience because it is so sparsely populated. Orient Beach is generally protected from the Atlantic by offshore reefs. The north end is where you will find more waves breaking around you. This is nothing like real surf but there is a little more action than you will find in the south end, which can approach millpond status some days. At either end, the water is warm and vivid with shades of luscious blues you'd swear had been photoshopped.

I had taken time on the south end to swim a little. It was, after all, my beach. The next solitary swimmer would have been well over a hundred meters away. The walk home was more of a stroll than a walk. I moved in and out of water as waves from the incoming tide lapped around my legs. It was not a moment to be rushed.

There is a change in dynamic once you reach Pedro's. It is the turning point. Once beyond Pedro's that clothing option is no longer an option as the morning matures. On that day, in particular, there were some early morning cruise people arriving in taxis behind Pedro's. When faced with a slew of options of what to see and do on their one day on this wonderful and varied Caribbean island, they had chosen to pack their cameras and head for the fringe of the nude beach to see if they could see someone without pants on.

As I crossed the line from unclothed to clothed, I tied on the small pareo that I had stored in my cap and then, with modesty intact, I headed north to mid-point of the beach where I had launched my day. Suddenly, it happened. Somewhere unseen in the water something had grabbed my foot. I tripped and stumbled forward, all my weight landing on my left foot that jammed into the wet sand and twisted. I had been snared by a loop of green rope that someone had anchored in the water. It all happened in fractions of a second, but the damage was done. I looked at my left foot. "Mon Dieu, mon orteil est cassé!" That poor toe sure looked broken.

It was my younger son who offered the first words of consolation. He was sorry about the toe and all that but said there was some comfort to be found in the timing. Imagine what might have evolved, he said, if the accident had happened in front of the camera-equipped cruise people on the other side of Perdo's. "Mature man makes crazy stumble on nude Caribbean beach." It would have been on uTube with over a million hits by the time I had made it back to the apartment.

Toes are just odd. Look at them one day. Closely. They are crazy wannabe fingers that are just not pretty. Do you know anyone that thinks toes are attractive or in some way sexual? If you do the odds are this is a court order floating around with his or her name on it. The big toe on my left foot was never what I considered one of my best features and now that it's a smear of red, blue and deep purple it hasn't gained any points but it has harnessed my constant attention.

There is a pharmacy nearby in Cul de Sac that we always visit. They have the coolest toothbrushes and the woman who runs it is very, very gracious and always remembers us. This time, we will be shopping for gauze, antiseptic solutions, and something for pain. Did I previously mention the pain? There were moments where it really, really hurt but now, if you don't pressure the toe to do anything it doesn't want to do, it's not bad. If anyone were to see the offending toe they would be sure to say how terrible it was and how much pain I must be in. I would simply nod, look brave and whisper "merci".

The jury is now out as to whether is toe is broken or not. It is so swollen it's very hard to tell. Next door to the pharmacy is a walk-in clinic. When you see the French name for a walk-in clinic is has different cachet, kind of Medicine Without Borders meets Hermes. You just know the dressings will be smart.

We have to wait. In the best traditions of anywhere hot where English is not spoken, people take their versions of siestas and languid lunches. Don't take that as a complaint; I think it's the smart way to live. When she arrives, Dr. Lillian Lafitte DuForte Montparnasse (Thinking about it now, I may have taken a liberty with the name) arrives. She is welcoming, a little vague, and very French. I can tell immediately from her profuse greeting in French that it was going to be a challenge for both of us. More smiles, More nodding. She quickly assumed that because I could say 'I don't speak French very well' with such a good accent that there was no need on her part to worry about language, and so she totally lost interest in attempting English.

I said I understood more than I should have but in the end, I walked away with a prescription for antibiotics and a laundry list of cleansing agents. She was lovely and lived to dispense kindness.

I could feel her passion for an essential oil that I was told to use to massage the toe. She was a little shocked that I didn't recognize the oil but that didn't smother her passion for it and she explained for perhaps the twelfth time how to massage the whole toe. Forget the drugs, bandage, cleaning agents for just a moment, the true essence of Dr. Lillian Lafitte DuForte Montparnasse's care and kindness would be found in the essential oil that she didn't actually prescribe. It was a very holistic encounter. My toe will be saved.

While we had waited for my Mini Medicine Without Borders to open, we had shopped at a nearby market. I think there is some correlation between personal judgment and emotional stability. I had been wounded. I needed comforting. This wasn't a time for low-calorie salads or tofu anything. I wanted something unhealthy. I wanted chips. When I saw a packet of chips that had 75% less of something it sounded like the perfect compromise. Sadly, the 75% less referred to taste. They were disgusting. Never mind, when we got back to the apartment, I had a healthy glass of red wine, looked out the window at the palm trees swaying on the rim of the turquoise waters and console myself that, one day, I would dance naked on the beach again.

Last night we went to Al Dente, an Italian restaurant in Cul de Sac. My wife's veal was under-seasoned and if this had been an episode of Chopped things would have been said. By comparison, my Spaghetti Carbonara was brilliant; all peppery and smooth and delicious; a much drier version than I had been used to. The pasta was cooked to perfection. Whoever did that pasta is definitely going on to the next round.

We had heavy rain last night. You could hear it pounding on the metal roof above us but it wasn't the rumbling of nature that woke me, it was the rumblings within me. I had been passing what felt like improvised explosive devices all morning. The only good news was that it took my mind off my toe for a while.

Madame Lafitte Et Cetera, my walk-in doctor, had said I should take the antibiotics for at least three days and then, if there was no sign of infection, quit them. I wasn't sure I could do that. I was totally convinced that the thunder down under was a direct side effect of the antibiotics. I did a little research, which confirmed my suspicion. There among the usual side effects like trouble breathing, trouble sleeping, trouble speaking, it euphemistically but clearly stated one might be blessed with spontaneously explosive bowels. Where were the other antibiotics, the nice ones that left you with a mild itch or a dry throat? Turns out my prescribed antibiotics were very French and only dispensed in a few select countries including Tunisia, and we know how picky they are. Why was I concerned?

At this point, I am feeling sure that the poor toe isn't actually broken just sadly mistreated. I am about to head out on a walk down the dirt road behind the beach. I may venture down to the beach itself if all bodes well. If I do nothing more than sit down and knock back a couple of

Caribs, it will be better than sitting home and whimpering. We shall see.

A day has come and gone and my dear toe has rallied. It's still gross but walking is way easier and I am heading out for a circuit with my wife. I am really looking forward to it. I did venture out yesterday but spent more time on sandy roads than on the beach itself.

Off to the beach itself this time! What's it like out there? Will it be 28C or will it have slipped to 27C? Should I wear a heavier t-shirt? Should I have a little more baguette first? What if the coffee is cold? These are the ways we now define stress.

Beaches are a great place for people watching. I love people watching almost as much as beach walking and if you can combine the two, bonus. I admit that sometimes my passion for watching people can perhaps cross a line. We are in a restaurant, I am sitting opposite my wife, we are talking, but my eyes slowly pan the room recording cool things I can use some day. I know it annoys my wife. I explain that I do it because I'm always a writer, she gives me a loving smile that clearly says no, it's because sometimes you're just a jerk. I would argue the point, but I would lose so I shut up.

We lay on lounges at La Playa and drifted in and out of life. Pretty idyllic. Just stretched out looking toward the distant edge of water and sky. I glanced to my right. There was a man two lounges over. He was reading a book. He had to be French; he was smoking. The thing that was totally captivating about him was his toes. My poor toes were permanently clenched with fear and trauma. His toes had been set free; they could fly. He would flex them, and they would spread, really spread wide open. He had toes like a freaking frog. I suffered serious toe envy. I couldn't take my eyes off them. I am sure that if he chose to, he could pick up things like screwdrivers or other small tools with them, or he could train them to operate small electrical appliances.

Fortunately, a fabulous woman released me momentarily from my toe fetish. She strolled in front of us like a shopworn showgirl. Damn, that woman had serious glitz. The glare was dazzling. It was like she had been in a Vegas club while they were cleaning out the wardrobe department. Every time they came across something even too tacky for Vegas, they would say "Get rid of it!" and she would shout, "No, no, give it to me, it's perfect for the beach." She proudly walked along the edge of the waters blithely blinding everyone in her path. She may have been totally crazy but she was having a good day.

Some people think that a clothing optional beach will be perhaps the most erotic thing to happen to them since high school sex. It just isn't like that. The truth is, I find it very asexual. Oh, it's very liberating, and it's the only way to swim in the ocean. All that is true but if you are hoping to see a cavalcade of perfect bodies it just ain't going to happen. The truth is that too many people have spent way more time in the drive through than at the gym.

I remember looking up Orient Beach to get some specific facts about the beach. There were ambient photos of what you could expect to see there. Oh, please. The two girls they featured had sun-kissed hair that caught the wind perfectly and bodies with maybe just three percent more body fat than a cadaver. They were not on the beach today.

They have never been on the beach. Any beach. Ever. That's not to say there aren't any attractive women on the beach. Of course, there are but they are real women, not fantasy images from glossy magazines.

Notable today were two guys who have been striding along the south end of the beach with immense confidence. They are in very good shape and marching in stride. The short one is fit. Really, really gay-gym fit, and he's proudly sporting one very commanding physical feature. When I said he was short I was referring to his height. If the rest of his body had conformed to conventional proportions when measured against his favourite body bit, this guy would be well in excess of nine feet tall.

We toss around the label 'clothing optional' as a polite way of saying you can probably take your pants off here, but it occurs to me that all beaches are actually clothing optional. It's measured by degrees. On your average beach, you have the option of wearing exactly what you want to wear, as long as you are wearing something. On your clothing optional beach, you just have that one critical extra option. Or not. On a true clothing optional beach, one of your options is to wear as many clothes as you like, and that is okay, too.

As I lay on my lounger watching the world stroll by on the slightly less optioned end of the beach, I became aware of what it was I was seeing as beach people came into view. I generally didn't see the person first; I tended to see what they are wearing. Could be a little, could be a lot but they were all carefully chosen labels, and they all had some statement or other to make. We've all done that, we've all laid out clothes for packing and thought about what do I think makes me look my best? We rarely buy clothes for exclusively utilitarian reasons. Down at the other end where the nude option is exercised, what do you first see when people approach? No, don't get ahead of me. I think the first thing you see the person. Period. Okay, then you may see some of the bits, but it's the person, him or herself who makes the impression not Tommy or Ralph or Giorgio or some other stranger we've come to depend on.

Other points of learning in life: tattoos. Walking on the beach can entrancing. Feeling the gentle warmth of your body, hearing the constant, individual rhythms of the waves, feeling the sand beneath bare feet. Now and then things drift into view, the focus locks and the impression is vivid. What the hell was that woman thinking to get those tattoos there? Often, you see tattoos placed at a certain height on the arm, close to a shoulder, centered on a calf. On this woman, they just sort of fell out of the sky, plop, with neither thought nor intuitive graphic sensibility. "How about there?" said the man with the tattoo gun as he wiped a little drool from his mouth with his free hand. "Oh, yeah!" said the woman with no comprehension. "And one more thing, Olaf," she said. "Can you make her ugly?" Okay, I total made that up that last bit. But man, the face of the woman on the back of that woman was just awful in every way. I thought that couldn't be an accident it had to be planned, but then I saw the ghastly galleon floating on the other half of her back and it all became clear. The dude with the gun couldn't draw shit.

How could this tragedy have happened? Probably it all traces back to Olaf, her tattoo artist, former seasonal farm worker, and RV maintenance assistant. One day Olaf drew a picture of a duck on the back of a beer coaster. It looked like a cow.

He showed it to his girlfriend who was still on the cusp of a three-day heroin haze. "Oh, man, that is beautiful," she said as she slipped off the barstool. "You are an artist, man, a true artist."

"Wow," said Olaf. "So many people said I could never be an artist, not with the lazy eye and the constant hand tremors." Buoyed by her enthusiasm, Olaf hurried home and ordered a Tattoo Gun Kit on Amazon for only $79.99 including express delivery. In just over one week after rendering a duck that looked like a cow, he was randomly defiling the beauty of the human body and people were paying him to do it.

By way of contrast, there was a guy on the south end of Orient Beach, the nude end, and he was something else. He had obviously worked on his body, and he was in great shape. He had one tattoo. Just one, but it extended from the nape of this neck to tops of his heels. It was amazing. Nothing had happened by chance there. It had been meticulously planned, and the whole body was a canvas on which a monochromatic pattern of wings and waves flowed in perfectly abstracted symmetry. I could barely imagine the patience of both the man and the artist. Who spawned the idea? How many times was it sketched out before ink touched skin? The result was extraordinary, beautiful. When I spoke to my wife about tattoo as art she said it was the finally the right time in my life for me to get that tattoo I kept talking about. I now have so much less time to regret it.

There I was considering tattoo as art when a squat, barrel-chested, man emerged from the waters. He, too, sported full body tattoos but his body was not a canvas, it was a demented sketchpad, a dire disarray of disappointing images and sadness. Any tattoo you could name, he had at least one of them, pudgy baby faces, bridges, trucks, rockets, wings, vines, wizards, witches, motorbikes, women on motorbikes, women in swimsuits, women with whips, a duck that looked like a duck, the ubiquitous barbed wire and so many more mistakes muddled into a blur of fading inks. He probably started his flesh gallery when he was much younger, with maybe one woman he thought was hot, then added, his car, a random dog and then it was too late to stop. Did he ever wonder if he would still love those choices some thirty years later? If he had seen even one of these images hanging in a gallery would he have bought it taken it home and hung it on a wall? Of course not. The only tattoo missing was the one that discreetly asked, "What the hell was I thinking?"

Tattoos are like copy squibs on book covers; they only hint at the actual content. It can be way too easy to define the whole person by bad choices of body art. Speaking of defining people badly, I am reminded of a time I spent working in Malta. Languishing in the Mediterranean, Malta is a very Catholic country, which is cool, except that it means there are no nude beaches on any of its three islands, Malta. Gozo or Camino. Well, that's not quite true. There is at least one and I found it. I spent six months working on the main island, Malta, and managed to make it to the beach almost every day. It was like a social club. Once Charlie, the social director, had recruited you to move rocks or rake sand, you knew you had been accepted. We would sit around in clusters discussing the elections in Croatia, the health of the Euro, who has the cheapest flights to Barcelona, and a host of the other critical issues that held life together.

Supplementing the core of regulars would be some day-trippers and tourists who might be regular visitors for up to a week at a time. One day in particular, I looked up to see a new person carefully maneuvering her way across the rocks that edged the beach. She was nude. Her skin was the colour of skim milk. She had to be English. She was the antithesis of the perky blondes on the beach brochure. She was adrift in a sea of cellulite. Her ample, loose body wrinkled and wobbled in every direction.

The point that must be made is that once I moved beyond any shallow and cruel first impressions and got to know the woman, she turned out to be utterly glorious in the most elevated sense of the word. Her eyes were brilliant mirrors of life. She had limitless passion. She was beautiful.

One day the conversation turned to Modigliani as it so often does in those places. I think he was a clue in a crossword puzzle or something. Somebody asked. “Does anyone know anything about Modigliani?” Our English friend smiled as if a memory she held dear had suddenly been rekindled. “Oh my, yes,” she said. “Poor Modigliani. Wasn't it sad that he should die so young, only thirty-five? He’d friends with Picasso after he’d moved to Paris in 1906, you know. They would drink wine together at Modigliani’s studio in Montmartre. Picasso would have to buy the wine of course.” And so the afternoon drifted into reflections of art, life in Paris, the lightness of air, the colour of water and the need for better local white wines.

Whatever you wanted to know you just had to ask. It was never a lecture; it was always a conversation. She was witty, wise and had an irresistible laugh. She knew exactly who she was and was content with that in every way. Each day after that first day, I would look for her, hoping she would come to the beach again even if only for an hour or two. I will never forget her and how beautiful she was. I am so much richer for having known her.

And she didn't have a single tattoo.

Born in Australia, Terry now lives in Canada with his wife, Donna. They have two sons and armfuls of grandchildren. Terry has acted extensively on stage and has written for the stage, television, film and print. *Matters of Kindness* is his first book of short stories. His novels, *Raising the Bar*, and *the printer, the actress and the cat she couldn't mention,* are slated for release in the latter half of 2016.

Kindness

terrybelleville.com

Going to the Dogs is an excerpt from my novel, Raising the Bar.

Made in the USA
Charleston, SC
22 August 2016